HECTOR

CHERYL
CHUMLEY

HECTOR

BOOK TWO OF CHLOE'S PEOPLE SERIES

CHERYL K. CHUMLEY

FIDELIS
PUBLISHING

Fidelis Publishing ®
Winchester, VA • Nashville, TN
www.fidelispublishing.com

ISBN: 9798992418637
ISBN: 9798992418644 (eBook)

Hector: A Novel
Book Two of the Series Chloe's People

Copyright© 2025 Cheryl Chumley

All rights reserved, including the right to reproduce this book or portions thereof in any form whatsoever. For information, address info@fidelispublishing.com.

No part of this publication may be reproduced or transmitted in any form or by any means electronic or mechanical, including photocopy, recording or any information storage and retrieval system now known or to be invented, without permission in writing from the publisher, except by a reviewer who wishes to quote brief passages in connection with a review written for inclusion in a magazine, newspaper, website, or broadcast.

This book is a work of fiction. Names, characters, places, and incidents either are products of the author's imagination or are used fictitiously. Any resemblance to actual events or locales or persons living or dead is entirely coincidental.

Scripture used in this book comes from the [I would prefer to keep the variety of Bible translations because not everyone uses the ESV. The Holy Bible, English Standard Version. ESV® Text Edition: 2016. Copyright © 2001 by Crossway Bibles, a publishing ministry of Good News Publishers.

Order at www.faithfultext.com for a significant discount. Email info@fidelis publishing.com to inquire about bulk purchase discounts.

Cover designed by Diana Lawrence
Interior design by Xcel Graphic
Edited by Amanda Varian

Manufactured in the United States of America

10 9 8 7 6 5 4 3 2 1

CHAPTER ONE

"Do it."

Hector stared down the alley at the red truck idling at the light and hesitated. He glanced nervously at his buddies. Leon's face was blank, expressionless, and his hand was steady as he held out the nine-millimeter, flat against his palm. Gio, next to him and swallowed by an overlarge gray hoodie, smiled broadly, his famously large teeth glinting white, even in the darkness. He slapped his hand lightly against his thigh, beating in time to some unknown song playing in his head. Hector cleared his throat and gulped. There would be no getting away from it. He nodded and took the gun, feeling the smooth black-and-silver of the barrel with his fingers before jamming it in his back waistband then pulling his sweatshirt down tight. He felt its cold against his skin and for a moment, had a terrible vision of it misfiring and sending a bullet into his spine.

His father's face flashed before his eyes and again, he hesitated. This is not how his father would want him to live.

"Come on bro. Before the light turns." Leon gave him a push for emphasis. "Gotta pay your dues."

Hector shook himself and took off at an easy pace down the alley, toward the street. Stepping from the shadows, he looked first to the left, then to the right, then again to the

HECTOR

left, and finally, at the windows of the truck. He scanned the occupants, just as he was taught.

The driver—male, wearing a brightly colored cap pulled low, was probably white. The passenger—female, youngish, maybe middle age, definitely white. He peered as best he could through the tiny window into the back seat but saw no other occupants. The woman's window was down a couple inches and he heard only the faint strumming of a guitar and a quiet male's voice, singing with an exaggerated twang so pronounced Hector grimaced.

He strode around the back of the truck to the driver's side door.

"Get out of the truck! Get out! Now!" He pounded his fist against the window and pointed his gun at the driver's head. The man turned his head, the bill of his cap concealing most of his face, then quickly, turned back to his passenger and reached for her. Dimly, Hector heard a woman scream.

The light turned green, Hector panicked, and punched the glass with the butt of his gun. It cracked and the driver pulled back in alarm. Furious, Hector wrapped both hands around the grip and held the barrel at the man's cap, keeping his eyes on the woman as he did, to make sure she wasn't trying to pull a gun or something out of her purse.

"Now! Get out!" He stepped back as the door started to crack open. He leaned around the driver and shouted at the woman. "You! Slide out this way! Let's go!"

The man stepped to the ground, his hands behind his head, his head swiveled to see his passenger. Hector shoved the back of his shoulder hard, causing him to stumble and then he waved the barrel of his gun toward the woman. She slid across the seat toward the driver's side, but before getting out, she stopped and fixed Hector with an angry glare. Hector paused, unsettled by the unexpected stare. Her eyes

CHERYL CHUMLEY

blazed and her lips pursed tightly and Hector watched in total disbelief as she raised her right hand sharply in the air. Her middle finger shot up straight and she wagged it back and forth few times just inches from his face. Then a wave of hot anger washed over Hector and he grabbed her roughly by the sleeve and yanked her to the ground.

"Get out! Now! Now! Now!" From the corner of his eye, he saw lights beaming from a side street.

"Hurry up! Get on the ground! Lay down, faces down!" He watched as the woman scurried to the man's side and they both dropped to the pavement, hands still behind heads, faces smashed onto the ground. The lights grew brighter.

"Don't you move an inch until you count to 1,000," Hector said, pushing the barrel onto the back of first the man's head and then the woman's, before jumping into the driver's seat of the truck. The passenger door opened and instinctively, Hector spun the gun to his right.

"Whoa, whoa, take it easy, man." Gio's massive teeth glinted in the light and with a sharp breath, Hector lowered his gun and Gio slid across the seat, followed quickly by Leon.

"Let's go man, let's go!" Leon slammed the door and Hector hit the gas pedal hard, headlights from an oncoming car flooding the cab. The wheels spun as he raced through the intersection, speeding through the next light and the next, before steering hard to the right, down a side street, then another, until nothing but black showed in his mirror when he checked to the rear.

Laughter filled the truck and Hector, in surprise, looked at his friends.

"Yo, you see that guy's face?" Leon opened his eyes as wide as they could go and then took two fingers of each hand and reached up and pulled them open even more.

3

HECTOR

Hector shook his head.

"No," he said. "He turned his face before I could see what he looked like. Why, what'd he do?" He kept quiet about what the woman did, though, and he chewed the inside of his cheek nervously as he remembered her stare. It was like she was memorizing his face and Hector knew Juan wouldn't be happy about that.

Or Romo, he groaned inwardly, vowing to never mention it.

"I thought he was gonna drop with a heart attack." Gio choked on his laughs and grabbed Hector's arm hard, as if to steady himself. "Oh man. You did good, though, bro."

"Yeah, you did it, man," Leon said, spreading his legs onto the dash and smiling broadly. He reached over and smacked Hector hard on the shoulder. "You one of us now."

Hector glanced sidewise at Leon but didn't return the smile. The thought didn't make him happy. After all, he'd been working alongside Leon and Gio for years now. He knew what they were like. He knew the darkness of their souls could one day become his. He bit his lip hard until he tasted blood and let the taste distract his mind from the distressing thoughts that sought to enter.

"Let's pull here for a while, bro, let everything clear," Leon said, pointing through the windshield. "Then we'll drop this with Juan."

Hector followed Leon's gestures and steered into an empty lot, pulling to the shadows of the tree line and shutting off the engine. He watched as Gio rifled through the glove box, pulling out papers and glancing at them, before crumpling them and tossing them out the window. He was about to tell Gio to stop, when Leon whistled, a long, drawn-out whistle, and all six eyes turned to look. Dangling from Gio's fingers was a long silvery chain, and dangling from the end of the chain was a sparkling silver object that gleamed and glittered as it danced.

"What the—" Gio held it still for a closer view. It was a silver Christian cross, dotted with delicate stones of red, yellow, blue, green, and white.

"Dude, are those diamonds?" Leon reached for the cross, but before he could take it Hector leaned over and snatched it from Gio's fingers.

"Gimme that," he said sharply.

It felt warm in his hands and he glanced at it with surprise. For a split second, a spark of light blinded him and he caught a strong, definite whiff of roses. Then the frightened face of the woman he just carjacked slid into mind, and it was as if he could actually hear her high-pitched scream right there in the cab, on the seat next to him. Startled, he shuddered and shoved the cross and chain deep into his front pocket.

"Hey, who says that's yours." It was a statement more than question, and Hector bit his tongue to hold back the first words that came to mind. He turned to Leon and shrugged, daring him with his eyes to try and take it. They stared that way for several seconds until Hector turned.

"Come on, dude," Hector said, putting his hands on the steering wheel and feeling the curves of leather with his fingers. "It's my first time. I gotta get something out of it." He hoped Leon would agree. The two had never before fought, but Hector had a sneaking suspicion Leon was stronger than he looked.

"Besides," he said, giving Leon a half smile and raising his eyebrow a bit, "whatdoya want a cross for? You're an atheist, man." He waited until Leon smiled back and then laughed.

"Yeah, keep it," Leon said, turning to the window.

HECTOR

Hector breathed a deep quiet sigh of relief. He had no idea why he wanted the cross so much, except maybe it reminded him of his mother and father. He leaned his head against the seat and reached down with his left hand and pinched the cross in his pocket, feeling its hardness and poking his finger into the points of the metal.

My father would not be proud, he thought, closing his eyes and remembering the face of his mother as she peered into his eyes and prayed a prayer of protection over his tired body each evening as he lay in bed.

And neither would she, he thought, his eyes growing damp with sadness.

✳ ✳ ✳

"Are you all right?"

There was silence for a moment, and he asked again.

"Chloe! Are you all right?"

She lifted her head and glanced toward the street, then strained her neck to both sides. The street was empty and she nodded, feeling slightly nauseous as her heart thumped hard against the pavement.

"James," she said, twisting her body into a seated position and waiting until he did the same. "They took your truck." She took deep gulps of air and swallowed hard, willing the nausea to pass.

"Well, you're not hurt, are you?" He stood and reached for her. Gingerly, using his arm as balance, Chloe pulled herself to her feet, then brushed her knees and the back of her pants.

"No. But we should call the cops." Chloe glanced down the darkened streets. "We should probably get out of here too." She watched as he felt in his pockets for something, then turned to her with hands lifted, palms open.

"They got my phone," he said.

Chloe sighed and shook her head.

"Aren't pastors supposed to be protected from this kind of thing?"

He looked at her and grimaced.

"It doesn't work that way, Chloe." He paused and took her by the arm, looking around then pointing at a group of street signs. "Let's head that way."

They walked in silence for several moments, their eyes peeled at the dark corners of the side streets and the black windows of passing buildings.

"So," Chloe said, with a light smile, "come here often?"

James chuckled, but his lips stayed drawn in a straight line. He looked at the abandoned row houses, their entrances boarded and covered in graffiti, and grabbed at her arm.

"Stay close, Chloe. We really don't know if anyone is behind those broken windows, watching us." He didn't finish the thought but squeezed harder on her forearm. Their footsteps sounded uncomfortably loud on the pavement, and unconsciously, they both tried stepping a little lighter as they went.

"Something just dawned on me, Chloe." He turned to her, frustrated. "Your mother's contact information was in my glove box."

"Oh, no." Chloe sighed and shook her head.

My long-lost mother, my long-lost mother, my long-lost mother, she thought. Just a couple hours ago, the idea of reaching out to the woman who gave her up at birth and then disappeared from the face of the earth seemed the most important moment of her life. James spent his own money

HECTOR

to hire a private investigator to track her down, and Chloe had more questions for her than she could count. But now, in the wake of a carjacking, she cared little about her mother.

After a moment, she asked, "But I suppose you can just go back and get the contact info again? Wherever it was you got it the first time?"

James suddenly dropped his hand from Chloe's arm and reached to his neck. He patted all around his chest, then checked each pocket in his pants and jacket, then reached under his jacket and felt for the pocket on his shirt.

"Oh no is right." He groaned loudly. "I'm sorry," he said, turning to her as if just hearing her questions. "You asked me something?"

"No, that's fine. I was just asking about the contact for my mother. Whether you can just get it again." She watched him curiously as he ran his hands through his pockets once more. "What's wrong, Jim?"

He groaned again and shook his head, his lips moving rapidly but silently, as if he were engaging in a tough verbal battle with himself.

"My cross was in the glove box too," he said.

Chloe looked at him, her eyes unblinking, helpless how to respond.

"It was white gold, had diamonds and other gemstones on it. Real gemstones. I mean, between the gold and the diamonds and the stones, it must be worth thousands. I never had it valued; I'm just guessing. But the diamonds alone . . ." he trailed off, his head shaking slightly. "The diamonds alone . . ." he said again.

Pastor James looked at her and gave another sigh.

"The real value was it was a gift, though." Chloe looked at him but said nothing. His face was downcast and he looked near tears.

"My uncle gave me that cross after he helped lead me to God. If it hadn't been for him, I never would have become a pastor. I never would have become a Christian, at least, not when I did. I probably never would've quit drinking." He raised his head and turned anguished eyes her way. "I'd be an alcoholic right now if it hadn't been for my uncle." His eyes narrowed as he looked into the distance. "And that cross was very special to me."

Chloe touched his shoulder gently and shook her head sadly. She was about to speak when he spun and faced her and grabbed both hands in his.

"Pray with me, Chloe. Pray with me now."

Surprised, she nodded and closed her eyes.

"Dear Lord," he said, his voice strangely loud in the empty street, "thank You for keeping us safe during these last minutes of terror. Thank You for letting us come from this attack unharmed, unhurt, mostly untouched—and it's due to Your heavenly protection, we know, that this is why we're unhurt right now. But Father, we ask You to please convict the ones who committed this crime of their sins. Don't let them sleep peacefully tonight, or any night, until they've turned from their path of evil, until they've repented from their acts of evil, and returned the properties they've stolen. Father, we ask specifically that You bring that cross and chain back safely and in one piece to us. You know, Father, how much that cross means to me." James paused, long enough that Chloe peeked and watched as he gulped deep, fighting to control his emotions. After a few moments, he went on and Chloe shut her eyes again.

"We ask, too, that You bring back the truck, Father. It is not mine. It is borrowed and my heart breaks at the thought of having to tell the owner it's been stolen. For his

HECTOR

sake, please, Father, convict these thieves and give them no peace until they've returned this truck."

James paused again, breathing deeply and squeezing Chloe's hands between his own.

"Father, it is Your teaching in the Bible that when Joseph was sold into slavery by his brothers, he did not later kill them when he had the opportunity but rather, forgave them and said that though they intended evil, God intended good—that out of their evil plots, God turned it for the good of Joseph, his family, and an entire population. And it is with that same spirit, Father, we say: We forgive these men of their crimes—"

At that, Chloe's eyes shot open.

Forgive them? She gasped, and James opened his eyes too. He regarded her evenly, then gave a nod and tightened his grip on her hands.

"Yes, Father, we forgive these men of their crime," he went on, waiting until Chloe shut her eyes and then closing his again. "Father, we ask that You use their sins against You for Your glory. We put the outcome of our requests into Your hands, we thank You again for saving us from harm and we praise You for sending Your Son, our Savior, Jesus Christ, to die for our sins so we may have everlasting life. It's in Jesus's name we pray, amen."

Chloe yanked her hands from James's grip.

"Why are your hands so hot? What the heck?" She rubbed them against her thighs.

"I know, mine got warm too," he said, blowing on the tips of his fingers. "That happens sometimes when I pray." They resumed walking. "I figure it means my prayers are being heard."

"Well, I don't know about that," she mumbled, her eyes on the ground, "but I do know forgiving people who hold guns to your head while they throw you to the ground and steal your truck—" she turned her head toward his and looked in his face, then continued, "and your cross chain that your uncle gave you—" she stared unblinking at his expression, then finished, "I do know forgiving people like that is definitely not in the Bible."

James laughed out loud, surprising Chloe. She tightened her lips and waited for him to explain.

"It *is* in the Bible," he said, still chuckling. "It's in a lot of places in the Bible. How about the part where Jesus teaches us how to pray—'forgive us our sins as we forgive those of our debtors'? Does that mean anything to you?" He smiled gently at Chloe's tight expression and patted her shoulder lightly. "We are to forgive others as Christ has forgiven us. And believe me, none of us are worthy of forgiveness. Not one. Not me, not you."

"And definitely not them," Chloe muttered, of the car-jackers.

They turned a corner and at the same time, gasped and ducked their heads. A flash of light, so bright they had to shut their eyes, beamed over them, and they stopped, waiting for the car to pass.

"Geesh," Chloe said, shaking her head hard. "Talk about blinded by the light."

James laughed, but Chloe refused to join him.

"I'll never forget that guy's face," she said, her voice hard. "The one with the gun, pointing it at you and then at me. I'll remember him until the day I die." She bit her lip hard, deep in thought. "And I hope the police have a good sketch artist," she finally said.

"Wouldn't matter to me if they did. I don't have a clue what he looks like. I didn't get a look at any of them."

HECTOR

Chloe turned to him with wide eyes. She was about to say something, then a strange expression came over her face and she stopped, her mouth formed in a small circle.

"Hey," she said, sniffing loudly, "do you smell roses?'

James sniffed, then nodded.

"I do. They're so strong, it smells like a rose garden out here."

CHAPTER TWO

"All right, let's go. It's clear."

Hector opened his eyes and gazed at the dark sky. A single star blinked, then seemed to disappear. He squinted hard but, try as he might, the light was gone. On impulse, he reached to his pocket and squeezed hard at the cross within the cloth folds. He didn't know why, but a wave a relief washed over him as his fingers felt the metal.

"Switch seats, Hector. I'm driving." Leon jumped from the truck before Hector could answer.

"I ain't being driven by no stupid kid." Leon pulled him by the shoulder, and Hector nearly stumbled onto the pavement.

"Hey!" Hector squared his shoulders and raised his chin. "I can drive better than you."

Leon smirked and waved him off, climbing behind the wheel and starting the engine.

"Sure thing, homie." He revved the engine. "You gonna walk or ride?"

Hector hurried to jump in and barely shut the door before Leon smashed his foot hard on the accelerator and raced across the lot into the street. He ran the first red light, then the second, then the third, and then they hit the highway.

HECTOR

"That's how you do it," he said triumphantly, glancing at his rearview mirror. "Don't give cops no time to catch up." He dug his shoulders deep into the seat until his back cracked. "Damn. This seat's more comfortable than my bed."

"You got a smoke?" Gio lifted his head and glanced at the road. "Where are we?" When nobody bothered to answer him, he let out a long sigh and smacked his fingertips on the dashboard, drumming to a tune only he could hear. "I *said . . .*" he repeated, drawing out his words and raising his voice, "anybody got a smoke?"

Hector felt in his pocket and pulled out a pack.

"Thanks, man," Gio mumbled, biting on the tip of the filter as he waited for the lighter. He let loose a long trail of smoke that stung Hector's eyes. As Hector rushed to crack the window, Gio chuckled and blew smoke his way again.

"Juan not gonna like how late it is," Gio said, looking to Leon for reply. Leon clamped his lips tight but said nothing. "I mean," Gio went on, not noticing Leon's knuckles as they gripped tighter on the wheel, "we was sposed to be there an hour ago. He's gonna wanna know whatsup."

Leon took his right hand off the steering wheel and slowly extended a middle finger until it stood ramrod straight. Then he moved his hand closer to Gio until it touched very lightly against his nose. Quickly, he bent his finger and hooked it under his thumb and in a flash, flicked it forward against the tip of Gio's nose. Gio howled and lowered his head.

"What the—" He rubbed his face frantically, trying to wipe away the sting.

Leon chortled.

"When I want to know what you think, I'll tell you. Otherwise, just shut the hell up."

They drove the rest of the way in silence, Gio sullen and nursing his nose every few seconds or so; Hector, quiet, his eyes fixed steadfastly out his window on the blackness of the night. His mind drifted to his father and a fishing trip they took near Colima when he was just a boy. It was one of those perfect days, the air clear and clean, and the sky so blue and cloudless it looked more like a painter's rendering than real. Even the breezes seemed perfectly timed. His father whistled, and their steps as they moved toward the water were in time with the tune. They actually laughed about that; how they were walking in sync with each other and with the song, without even thinking, as if in the military. That's when his father turned toward him with such suddenness Hector nearly dropped his fishing gear.

"Stay away from the military, son. It's no career for you."

Hector, taken aback by the sudden switch in his father's demeanor, could only nod in reply. He gazed at his father's unblinking eyes. Then, as if nothing had happened, his father patted him on the head and smiled.

"Good boy." He began whistling and walking again.

It was some time later, after casting their lines and unpacking the empanadas they saved from the previous night's dinner, Hector realized he hadn't asked why. He turned to his father, the question on his lips. But then his pole moved and his line pulled tight and in the excitement of reeling, he forgot to ask.

It wasn't long after that he learned the answer. It was the moment his life changed irrevocably and for the worse.

Bitterness stabbed at his heart and Hector shook away the memory. *The past is the past*, he thought. *The present is the present*. His mood only darkened as they drew nearer to home.

HECTOR

Home was a generous word. It was the place Hector had been whisked to years ago, shut up and imprisoned. He had been only ten, tiny for his age and terrified, and his first impression then of the house was a physical reaction to its stink. It was an odor of decaying food and spoiled milk, and when Hector glimpsed the kitchen, he understood why. Flies buzzed about a stack of dishes in the sink, landing periodically on a plate, on a cup, on a spoon. The sight sickened him then and still did now.

But it was home. Or at least, it was the place he was forced to call home.

Hector's body rocked gently as Leon navigated the bumpy unpaved lane leading to the building. It stood small and unwelcoming, a ghastly dirty yellow shape illuminated against a dark night by an even dirtier yellowed single bulb dangling precariously from a metal pole. The exterior was stucco mixed with ugly patches of dirt and mud. On the porch, that is, on the slab of cement supposedly serving as a porch, was a round scuffed silver bowl out of which spilled bits of white. From a distance, the white looked like a sampling of cloth, perhaps a forgotten scarf or stray sock. Hector knew they were cigarette butts—dirty, disgusting, browned cigarette butts with stamped ends that left telltale marks on the siding of the house where they had been extinguished, before being dropped carelessly to the ground. The red paint of the door cast an eerie tint in the yellow of the bulb, and Hector shuddered, thinking of blood.

They drove past the front into the back and Hector caught a quick movement between the broken slats of the window blinds,

Leon must have noticed as well.

"He's up." Leon braked sharply, sending Gio into the dash. Ignoring Gio's angry response, Leon yanked out the key from the ignition and shoved open his door.

"I need your counts," he said, one foot dangling toward the ground, the other still on the brake pedal. He held out his hand, palm up, and wagging his fingers impatiently.

Hector raised his hips from the seat so he could dig deeper into his pockets. He pulled out a wad of bills and with barely a glance, dropped them into Leon's hand. Gio did the same, and Hector turned away in disgust, as he always did when it was time to turn in his money. His father used to tell him stories about the drug dealers he'd regularly arrest and about the lost souls who wandered the streets at night in search of their next fix, and how utterly unconcerned the dealers were about the lives they destroyed. "They're the scum of society," his father would say, "lower even than pond scum." And now Hector was forced to be one of them.

His face flushed hot at the thought and he bit his tongue to keep from exploding on Leon.

"Let's go." Leon's voice was sharp and he smacked Gio on the shoulder for emphasis.

Their feet crunched loudly in the darkness as they made their way to the front door. Leon rapped sharply twice then softly once on the front door, then with hand on knob, waited. The door flew open and Leon jumped back so fast he knocked Gio off the porch.

"You're late."

It was spoken quietly but with such ferocity, Hector shivered. He had only met Juan on two prior occasions, and on both he had the same involuntary reactions. The sheer mass of Juan's body filled the doorway; he was more squat than tall, with a neck that seemed as if it were formed of a boulder and set in concrete upon broad shoulders. His head

HECTOR

was squared, bordered by smooth black hair clipped tight and jagged. His brows were bushy and oily and black—the same black as his head but more greasy than hairy, like the coat of a bear emerging from water—and they gleamed in the yellow of the light above two glittering dark holes that were his eyes. Hector could only glance at those eyes for a second or two at a time. Anything longer and he would feel a coldness in his stomach, winding toward his heart.

"We had to wait for the cops to clear."

Leon's voice was soft and cautious, as if he were speaking to a man holding a gun.

"Cops?" Juan's eyes swept over the three, then with a quick movement, quicker than someone of his size would seem capable of making, he turned and waved over his shoulder.

"Let's go."

He pointed to a couch just inside the front door and without a word, they took their seats: Leon first, on the end, then Gio on the other end, then Hector, rather uncomfortably, in the middle. Hector put his hands on his knees and watched nervously as Juan disappeared down a hallway and into the dark. Gio tapped his foot lightly, his knee bouncing slightly against Hector's leg. Hector was about to tell him to stop when Juan came back into the room. In his hands were four bottles, two in each. Hector took one and with a mumbled "thanks," held it tightly against his lap. Leon and Gio sucked deeply at theirs as Juan plopped into a chair directly across the couch, and for several seconds, silence ensued. Then Hector felt an elbow digging into his side and with a start, he looked up and saw Juan glaring at him. Quickly, he lifted his bottle and took a long drink. The beer was warm and bitter tasting and he fought the urge to cough.

Satisfied, Juan turned expressionless eyes to Leon.

"What's these cops you were talking about?"

Leon cleared his throat and waved his hand dismissively.

"Nothing. There weren't any cops. But just in case, we waited for the roads to clear."

"So you lied?" His voice was without expression, and Hector felt the hair on his arms rise.

"No! No no no no." Leon held up his hands, one still holding the beer bottle, defensively. "I figured they was gonna call the cops. Just in case they called the cops, I wanted to hide out a bit. Y'know, wait for the coast to clear and all."

Juan sat immobile, and for several tense seconds Hector held his breath, thinking of a nature show he once watched where the leopards went perfectly still right before they pounced. Then Juan cracked a slight smile, a golden incisor flashing in the dim light.

"Smart." He lifted his bottle and with what seemed one single long swallow, drained its contents. He dropped it on the floor with a clatter, then stood.

"Go put it in the shop now. I'll meet you around back." He turned to Gio. "You go with him."

Hector was suddenly alone, and he sat for several minutes in nervous stillness, barely moving except for sporadic lifts of his arm to bring the bottle to his lips, followed by slight scowls as he forced the swallows. When he got the bottle to half empty, he figured that was good enough and gingerly, so as not to knock it over, he placed it on the floor alongside his feet. After another minute or two of waiting, he turned his head and craned his neck down the hallway. Restless, he stretched, his foot mistakenly hitting the bottle. He caught it before it tipped and decided the best course of action would be to pour the rest of the beer down the sink then throw it away. Seeing no sink and no trash barrel, he

HECTOR

decided he might find both at the end of the hallway, so after a quick glance out the front window, he headed into the inner parts of the house.

He saw dimly what seemed to be a light switch and flicked it. Something moved to his right and Hector jumped, then watched as a mouse scurried across the countertop and disappeared behind the stove. The sink was piled with dirty dishes and a smell of rotted flesh filled his nose. Cupping a hand over his mouth and squeezing his nostrils with two fingers, he searched for a trash barrel. Finding none, he decided to place his half-empty bottle on the counter, between a pile of plates with visibly hardened crusts of food and a mountain of empty cardboard boxes, a couple of which oozed some sort of brown sauce. He set down his beer and stepped back. He doubted Juan would notice.

A loud shout came from the yard area where they had parked the truck, and curious, Hector flicked off the light before cracking open the back door. He heard muffled voices and stepped into the night air. He caught sight of a bright light through the tree line and peering closer, he saw a larger building, located about fifty feet away. It was partially concealed by trees and brush, and except for the light, he probably wouldn't have noticed it at all. Once again, the sound of muffled voices drifted to him, followed by the distinctive sound of Gio's crazed laugh. He walked quietly toward the sounds, turning his head this way and that, dreading the idea of Juan's face suddenly popping in his pathway.

He saw a window on the side propped partially open and he slipped quietly beneath it to listen. Then his eyes fell on a pile of cement blocks just a few feet away and grabbing one, he placed it under the window and stepped on it. It was just high enough to boost his eyes above the window ledge. He peered inside, blinking several times until his eyes adjusted to the bright lights hanging from the ceiling, and saw with some surprise the floor was littered with car parts. A half dozen cars in various states of wreckage, some on lifts with their wheels removed, were scattered about the room. A man in a gray jumpsuit was busily yanking something from beneath the hood of what was left of a maroon-colored Cadillac. Hector squinted at a stack of boxes to the Cadillac's left, trying to read the labels in black marker. He caught the letters "CCs" on one and after a moment, decided it stood for catalytic converters.

A shout came from right below his window, just out of his line of sight, startling Hector so much he almost lost his balance and fell. He recovered, though, then listened with growing alarm at the conversation on the other side of the wall, seemingly right beneath his feet.

"You better be glad you didn't break that." Juan's deep voice was unmistakable, and Hector pulled back slightly from the window, checking that his shadow wasn't giving him away.

"Yo dog. I got it. Here it is." Leon sounded a lot more relaxed than he had in the house, and Hector wondered if the beer was having an effect.

Hector strained to hear and, after a few seconds of silence, he caught a jumble of sounds, strangely muffled as if they were compressed in an airtight container. Intuitively, he cocked his head and as the sounds grew louder, he realized he was listening to a playback of audio or video. With a jolt of surprise, he heard his own voice—"Now! Now! Now!"

It was the carjacking and as he strained to listen, a chill raced down Hector's spine, partly from the memory of his own violent behavior leading to the panicked expressions on

HECTOR

the faces of the man and woman he accosted, and partly from the shock of realizing his actions had all been recorded—and now the recording seemed to be in the possession of a man he greatly loathed and feared.

With a lunge Hector pushed as far forward against the window as he could. His eye caught a movement to his left and looking over, he saw reflected in the side mirror of one of the cars the figures of Juan and Leon. Their heads were bent, as if focused intently on something in their hands. The pair shifted slightly in their stances, just enough for Hector to make out the small black cell phone in Leon's hand.

His heart skipped a beat. He didn't know why Leon and Juan would want a recording of the carjacking, but he knew it couldn't be for anything good.

"Good job, Leon. Nice and clean. Go download it for me in my office. Then come see me. You and me gotta talk his next test. If he don't pass loyalty, then he ain't no use."

Hector slipped from the window ledge and dropped lightly to the ground. Carefully, he picked up the concrete block and wiped it lightly to remove any dirt, before returning it to its original position. His chest felt tight as he mulled Juan's words.

He was talking about killing; Hector couldn't see any other loyalty test after a carjacking besides a killing. Hector looked deep into the darkness, trying to make out a horizon line in the distance. It was too black to see one. But he knew it existed and for a split second, he almost ran. Then a slam from behind him made him jump, and he raced to the back door of the house and slipped inside. Quietly, he shut the door behind him and moved back to the couch. He was just settling his body in what he hoped was the same position as before he left when the front door smashed open so loudly he jumped to his feet.

Juan sneered at him then glared.

"What you so jumpy for, amigo."

"Nothing!" Hector fought the urge to shout again. "Nothing," he said, forcing himself back to the couch and turning his head from Juan's eyes. He found it difficult to maintain contact with the dark holes and he reached to the floor, feeling about for his bottle. Then he remembered he poured it out and put it in the kitchen and, once again, he panicked. He felt sure Juan, just by staring, would figure out he had left the living room and then it would just be a matter of time before he would guess Hector overheard a conversation he was not meant to hear. Awkwardly, Hector fished about the floor with his hand, then pulled it back sharply into his lap, where he set it alongside his other, palms flat on his legs. His eyes flitted nervously as Juan dropped into his chair and regarded him for several long moments in silence. Hector felt his forehead warm then grow wet, but he dared not lift his hand to wipe the sweat.

Finally, Juan spoke.

"I'm gonna ask you something and I'm gonna give you just one chance to tell me the truth."

Hector's eyes shot to Juan, and they grew wide in alarm at his expression. Juan's face was expressionless, like a cold statue on a snowy hill, with black slits of ice for the eyes. He stared and the more he stared, the more Hector felt his forehead dampen and then he fought so hard to keep his face from giving away his secret, his nose turned numb. He opened his mouth to speak, but found his tongue was swollen and wouldn't move.

"No bro, don't say anything. Just lissen."

Hector nodded, relieved. He worked on his breathing, counting four in and four out, four in, four out, keeping

HECTOR

his eyes fixed at the bridge of Juan's nose, right at the spot between his eyes.

"I wanna know why you stole from me."

Hector's head shot back in surprise and he dropped his jaw, forming a large circle with his lips. He gasped, and was about to say something, then his fingers felt at his pocket and with a sudden dread, he snapped shut his lips. He dropped his eyes and held his breath, fear seizing his heart. Slowly, he reached into his pocket and pulled forth the chain and cross. Without raising his head, he held out the chain in his cupped hand.

"Here." He waited in the silence, not daring to meet Juan's gaze. "I didn't steal it, I swear. I was holding it for you." He shook it lightly, as if emphasizing his words. "It's all yours."

Hector heard rather than saw Juan's massive body lean forward and he squeezed his eyes tight, waiting for the blow, tensing his shoulders in anticipation. Instead, he felt the soft touch of a hand on his hair and he looked up in surprise and wonder. Juan was towering over him, peering down deeply into his eyes. Hector held his breath, trying in vain to guess Juan's intentions. Juan flashed his teeth then just as quickly, shut his lips.

"You keep it, bro. This time. But don't you ever steal from me again."

Hector nodded enthusiastically, overwhelmed with relief. He'd seen Juan's anger firsthand before and he had no desire to experience it again. Then Juan bent and leaned close and for a chilling second, Hector thought he'd changed his mind. The smell of beer flooded Hector's nostrils and he struggled to maintain his composure as Juan's breath blew hot against his ear.

"Yo, you really smacked it to Gio over *this*?" Juan straightened and burst into choppy laughter, slapping Hector on the shoulder before turning toward the hallway. Hector forced a smile, then a laugh, gulping deeply and quietly—he hoped. Juan's voice turned flat again.

"Seriously, man. You wanna keep that cause you religious or something—that's fine. But you gotta know the right religion. You gotta get good with the right god. I got a church for you. Tomorrow." Juan blinked black eyes, then turned and walked a few steps. From the darkness of the hallway, his words seemed more warning than anything.

"Tomorrow, bro. We go to church."

Hector unfolded his fingers and gazed at the chain in his palm, tapping it lightly to try and catch a bit of its glitter. But it was too dark. The cross lay flat in his palm, a piece of cold, dark metal.

CHAPTER THREE

"Wake up, man. Get up."

Hector grunted and yanked his shoulder away, burrowing both arms deep into the couch cushions beneath his body. In his half-sleep state, his normal internal alarm bells were muted. A sudden shove snapped open his eyes and with a thud, he found himself on the floor.

"I said get the freak up." It was the voice of Leon, and for emphasis he followed the command with a kick.

"Oww!" Hector, fully awake now, rubbed his elbow and leaned back against the couch. He stretched his long legs and reached to tie his boot. He used to take his shoes off to sleep, until he learned his lesson the night the cops raided Leon's home in the dead of winter and they were forced to jump out the window to flee. Hector, barefoot and wearing only shorts, nearly froze to death in the woods, waiting for the all-clear. What made it worse was Leon's refusal to share any of his own clothing items. Hector shivered and watched as a warmed Leon zipped down his coat to expose a thick hoodie, which he also unzipped and flapped in the air, as if fanning an overheated body. Each minute brought new agonies for Hector and he alternately ran in place and did jumping jacks, furiously rubbing his feet and hugging his arms tightly as he glared at Leon, reclined comfortably against a tree. Later, back at the house and wrapping

HECTOR

as many blankets around his shoulders as he could find, Hector laced into Leon.

"I coulda died," he told him.

Leon had just smiled and raised his middle finger.

"It's a lesson, dude. That's called a life lesson."

It was one Hector never forgot. As if reading his mind, Leon kicked at Hector's boot.

"I guess you still remember that night cops raided us." He smirked at Hector's scowl. "Yeah, man, I did you a big favor. Remember that."

"Sure. I owe you," Hector said sarcastically, sliding his body to a seated position on the couch. He watched the dirt float in the ray of sunshine peeking through the slats on the window. "Why you waking me?"

Leon plopped into the chair where Juan had sat the previous evening.

"Juan wants you up. He says he taking you to church today." Leon snorted as he said the word "church," and Hector looked up sharply. He knew better than to ask, though. Leon never explained what he meant.

"Go meet him out back," Leon said, leaning his head back against the chair and shutting his eyes. He folded his arms across his chest and sighed deeply. Hector watched him breathe, chewing the tip of his middle fingernail lightly and reflecting on the words of last evening. His body rocked lightly and he fought the urge to pace.

"He ain't gonna tell you twice."

Startled, Hector jumped to his feet. Leon was staring at him through slit eyes, so narrow they looked like two little paint strokes. Instead of going out the front, Hector walked down the hallway, hoping to find something in the fridge to eat. He grabbed a box of crackers off the counter, and peering in the refrigerator, found a can of cheese in the back. He shook it and angled it toward his face, pressing lightly on the tab. A line of yellowish orange mush oozed into his mouth and he smacked his lips with satisfaction.

Juan was in his truck behind the driver's wheel, and Hector hurried to get in beside him. Juan's truck was green and rusty with a torn vinyl front seat that spit out yellow foam. The floor was littered with trash, and Hector's feet kicked at several paper bags from various fast-food restaurants as he slid into place. A blast of warm air hit him in the face and Hector shifted his head a couple inches to the left. The vent, he knew, didn't close and the heater was stuck on high.

"Gimme one of those." Juan nodded toward the box of crackers. Hector held up the can of cheese. "Nah," Juan said, pulling down the dirt road toward the street. Without looking, he accepted the small pile of crackers from Hector's hands.

"You gonna like this." Crumbs blew from Juan's mouth as he spoke and instead of swallowing, he shoved two more crackers into his cheeks and chewed furiously. "It ain't like any church you ever been to before, I bet."

Hector just nodded, not sure how to answer. He actually didn't have that much experience with church. His parents weren't overly religious and only went to service on special occasions, but they did believe in God. His mother prayed with him every night. "Now Hector," she would say, "make sure you always thank God first, before you ask Him for anything, and then you thank God last, before you shut your eyes." She would sit there on the edge of his bed and listen as he listed off the things he was thankful for, and if he finished too early, she would prod him until he added more. "What about your dinner?" she would say. "Aren't you grateful you're not going to bed hungry tonight?" Then Hector

HECTOR

would thank God for dinner, and for the food on the table, and the drinks in his cup, and the leftovers in the kitchen. "What about that blanket that's covering you right now?" she would add. "Aren't you thankful you aren't laying there shivering?" Then Hector would thank God for the blankets and the pillows and the bed and his pajamas, and then if his mother stayed silent, and seemed to be waiting, he would go on and thank God for the toothpaste and his toothbrush, so he could clean his teeth, and the cup he filled with water to rinse his mouth after he brushed his teeth, and the towels he washed and wiped his face with as he readied for bedtime each evening. Then he would open his eyes and peek at his mother; if she was smiling, he knew the prayers were finished. She would pat his arm gently, and they would always finish the same way: "In Jesus's name, we thank You for all."

Hector couldn't remember when the nighttime prayers with his mother began; it seemed they had always been a part of his life. But he remembered when they stopped. The night the cartel gunmen came to his home to kill his parents was the last time Hector said his bedtime prayers. There just didn't seem to be much to thank God for after that.

Hector glanced at Juan without saying a word, then turned to the window to hide his expression. His eyes burned with hate, and fury coursed through his veins as he dug his nails deep into his palms to keep from screaming.

"Am I right, Chico?" Juan laughed a humorless laugh and punched Hector on the shoulder. Then his voice turned chilling, and Hector swallowed hard, knowing he'd have to say something. "I asked you a question, Chico."

Hector turned to Juan with a tight smile, and hoped his eyes wouldn't give him away.

"You right, Juan." He nodded for emphasis. "I doubt I been to a church like this before."

Juan narrowed his eyes, and for a second, Hector's heart beat faster. Then the right front wheel edged slightly off the side of the road, striking a pothole, and Juan and Hector grabbed at the dash to steady themselves. Juan cursed as he pulled the wheel hard to the left. He glanced in his mirrors, then to Hector, and laughed, a loud, maniacal laugh that somehow seemed more menacing than even his glares.

"You should see your face," he said, laughing again as Hector pulled down the visor above his head and looked at his reflection. He was glad for the excuse. Dull eyes, the kind that came with practice, say by repeated run-ins with police on the street, stared back at him and he sighed lightly with relief. He felt a pain in his right palm and noticed with some surprise he was still digging in his nails. He relaxed his grip and rubbed hard at his cheek, wiping away any remaining expression. Then with a quick flick of his fingers, he snapped the visor into place and reached for the crackers that had fallen to the floor. Pulling out three, he sprayed them with cheese and popped them into his mouth, one after the other, chewing and swallowing in almost one smooth motion.

"We're here." Juan pulled to the right and parked along the street curb, right behind a beat-up Jeep with a license plate so caked with dirt, only the letter K showed, and partially, the number 7. Hector looked around with surprise.

"Where?" The street was empty except for a few parked cars in front of crumbling houses with boarded-up windows and lopsided porches. At first glance, they appeared abandoned. But then Hector noticed a woman seated by her front door, staring at them as she blew streams of smoke from her mouth, and as he followed the trails in the air from her cigarette, his eyes fell on a bony black and tan dog in the next yard. It was chained to a post poking out

HECTOR

of a patch of dried and yellowed grass, and it didn't move, except for its eyes which followed Hector as he stepped from the truck. He stared back and wondered how long it had sat there, more a statue than live. A loud bang from somewhere down the street made him jump and he perked his ears at the sound of a man's shout and a baby's cries. He watched as the man, dressed in ripped blue jeans and a black plaid patterned hoodie, stormed across the yard to his car then yank hard at the driver's side handle. When it wouldn't open, the man began to kick furiously at the door. Even from that distance, Hector could see the dents the man's boots left on his car. With a final kick, he gave up and stomped down the road, disappearing from view between a chest-high pile of trash bags in the street and the side of a house, half painted yellow and the other half brown.

"Let's go, man." Juan grabbed him by the shoulder and shoved him up the sidewalk, toward a rickety house with dark shades over the windows.

Hector scrunched his nose in confusion.

"I thought you said we were going to church."

Juan shot him a look over his shoulder as he climbed the steps to the porch. He lifted his foot gingerly over a hole in the wood the size of a small bowling ball.

"This is."

He turned the doorknob without knocking and stepped inside, waiting for Hector to follow. Hector looked with wonder at a bevy of statues placed tightly together around a table in the corner, lit up by a collection of candles of various colors and shapes. The first statue he noticed was draped in a bright red cloth, a loose hood billowing about its skeleton face. He looked quickly at the other statues and saw with shock they were all skeletons, each draped in different colored coverings, each holding in a bony hand a large scythe with a curvy blade stretching high into the air. Hector peered closer at the table and as his eyes adjusted to the candlelight, he saw it was littered with stacks of cash, small shot glasses filled with golden liquid, a bottle with a label he couldn't quite make out but recognized as some sort of liquor, several packs of cigarettes—with one lit, its white butt wedged tightly in the groove of a green ashtray—and an untold number of multicolored strands of beads and scarves. He sniffed and a sweet fruity odor filled his nostrils. He traced the smell to the front window sill where several sticks of incense burned.

"Juan."

Hector turned toward a man with a bulbous face and dark skin, dressed in a flowing white robe. Long chains hung from his neck and his head was covered with a triangular shaped cone of gold. It reminded Hector of the head covering worn by the Catholic Church's pope, only much more garish.

"Romo." Juan stepped to embrace the man, kissing him lightly on both cheeks before bending to kiss a large gold ring on his left hand. It was embedded with the largest ruby Hector ever saw and its blood red flickered in the candlelight, sending little flashes of color onto Juan's face. Hector shivered, feeling suddenly cold.

"And who's this?" Romo's voice was quiet but commanding and his teeth flashed white, not unlike a wolf sending a warning. Hector saw very little difference between Romo's eyes and those of the dark sockets on the skeletons propped around the table.

Hector was loathe to take the hand that extended his way, but he didn't want to offend so he tentatively wrapped his fingers in Romo's grip.

"His name's Hector."

HECTOR

Romo didn't just shake his hand; he pulled on his arm and Hector felt himself drawn close, just inches from his face. Romo's stale breath poured over him like an unwelcome pant from a dog, and Hector fought the urge to turn his head in disgust.

"Hector."

Romo squeezed tight on Hector's fingers and leaned in even closer, until the tips of their noses almost touched. Hector froze, confused and a bit fearful at the unexpected intimacy. Romo's eyes were deeply set and rimmed in wrinkled skin with a reddish hue, ghastly but strangely hypnotic. For a few short moments, or maybe it was hours, Hector stared deep into those eyes and as he did, the surrounding objects in the room receded then disappeared. Then the eyes became meaningless circles, black but without definition, and within the center of the two black circles, where the irises should have been, glowed nearly imperceptible fiery lights. Hector gazed as if in a trance, trying to bring the lights into focus. The dots didn't blink but seemed to grow larger—larger and blacker until they enveloped Hector in a tight, dark embrace and he lost all sense of his own body. He couldn't move, he couldn't even think of moving, and as his feet started to tingle and then lose contact with the floor, all Hector could see was the darkness and within the darkness, the set of unblinking lights the size of a pinhead and the color of glowing, hot embers. He thought he should be afraid but instead, felt warmth course through his body.

From the darkness, from afar, came Juan's voice. With a jolt, Hector was back in the room with the dark eyes of skeletons dancing merrily as they mocked him from their spots by the candles.

"He's the one we told you about."

CHERYL CHUMLEY

"Ahh yes," Romo said, stepping back and flashing another smile. Hector blinked hard, searching Romo's face for clues into what had just happened. But Romo simply smiled again and with a quick pump of his arm, he shook Hector's hand and let it drop. Hector's mouth dropped open as he saw two blue eyes peering back at him.

"Do you have prayers for the Skinny Lady?"

Hector smiled weakly, unsure how to respond. Romo's blue eyes were making him uncomfortable and he glanced at Juan with a silent plea.

"That's why we're here."

Romo clapped Juan on the back then pulled his head close. Hector watched Romo's lips move just inches from Juan's ear, but he couldn't make out what was said. But when the two turned tilted heads his way and fixed him with narrowed eyes, he felt again a shiver run through his body. The whole place was giving Hector the creeps and he glanced toward the front door, trying to imagine their response if he just ran and ripped it open and fled down the street. Then Juan was guiding him toward the table with one hand tightly on his shoulder and the opportunity passed.

"On your knees," Juan said, pushing Hector to the floor before bending next to him.

To his left, Hector saw Romo lay a clean golden bowl on the table before them, then pull a knife from within his robes and lay it by the bowl. Romo stepped back and disappeared down a dark hallway, and when Hector turned back to Juan, he saw the knife in his hand. Nervously, Hector shifted on his knees.

"What's up now," he said, glancing from the knife to Juan's face to the skeleton figures standing before them, then back to the knife. Juan's eyes darkened and he leaned in close and whispered. Hector's face turned white and he

35

HECTOR

drew back sharply but he was too late. Juan's fist closed tight over his wrist and he firmly pulled it until it was positioned directly over the bowl. Confused and frightened, Hector tugged, but he couldn't soften Juan's grip. Silver flashed and a second later, red poured forth, and with shock Hector watched as blood flowed from his hand into the golden bowl. The dark liquid spread and covered the entire bottom. Horrified, Hector watched as Juan wiped the blade of the knife on a piece of white cloth he then tucked carefully into the belly of the bowl. Red soaked up the side of the cloth, a ghastly bath of blood, and Juan placed both hands together in front of his chest, palms open, and began to mumble in an almost cadence, rocking gently back and forth in time to his words.

Hector sat silently, clasping his sliced hand with his other and pushing hard at the mound on his palm to try and dull the pain.

After a few minutes, Juan stopped mumbling, raised his head, and glanced at Hector's hand, which was still dripping blood, then pulled a dirty cloth from his pocket and tossed it on the floor between them.

"Wrap it tight, amigo." Juan turned back to the table and lifted his head high to the figure draped in black, the one holding in one hand a scythe and the other, a globe. Reaching forward, Juan picked up a black candle and then a gold candle, lit them both, and placed them carefully at the feet of the black-hooded skeleton. He dropped his head to his chest and began to mumble once again. Hector, without realizing, began to rock slightly in harmony with Juan. His hand throbbed, but there was something mystical about the way the black eyes of the hooded statues seemed to stare right through him, and the more he looked at their faces, the less frightening they appeared. Between the flickering of the candles and the dancing of the shadows, and with the rhythmic babbling playing in the background, Hector began to relax and he dropped shoulders he hadn't even realized were tightened. He breathed deeply, letting the dreaminess seep all through his body. He felt at peace—a peace that surpassed all understanding! He smiled as the phrase from a long-ago time floated into his mind. For the first time in a very long time, Hector felt at home and the confidence gave him courage to peek at the figures to his front.

Shadows swirled and black eyes stared and for a brief glorious moment, the black-hooded figure turned a broad smile toward Hector. It wasn't a frightening grin either—all bones and teeth and darkness—but rather one full of recognition and promise, the type of smile a loved one reserves for a friend who's gone missing for years, and who is suddenly at the front door. For the second time since entering the house, Hector felt warmth flood his body and he nearly laughed out loud at the shiver of excitement springing from his spine and running up the small of his back. His mind filled with images of riches and joy—of golden chests of gold and of eager, excited faces of friends who danced in carefree circles around a softly glowing fire pit. He let his hands drop to his lap, opened his eyes wide, and focused with calm detachment at the bright red cloth in the bowl. He tried for several moments to remember why that red cloth caused him so much pain and fear earlier—he even squinted hard, narrowing his gaze at the bowl while rubbing absently at his bandaged hand. But it was a distant memory. His mind was jelly, and he gave up the mental quest. It didn't matter, anyway, he decided. She was there and everything was fine. In fact, he thought, glancing reverently into the skeletal face of his new friend, everything was better than fine.

HECTOR

"She'll protect you if you ask her."

Romo's voice was an echo, and Hector barely turned at the touch on his shoulder.

"She says your blood's not enough, though."

Hector nodded, first lightly, unwilling to abandon his dream state and hoping Romo would go away.

"Your blood's just the beginning," Romo said.

Hector squeezed his eyes tight, trying to recapture the feeling, but it was no use. The warm was gone. He propped open his eyes and glanced at Romo with annoyance. Then he peered again to the eyes of the black-hooded skeleton, searching for the spark or at least a semblance of the spark that brought him such special feelings, hoping against hope it hadn't all been in his imagination. But the eyes had turned dark and unseeing, circles of black, offering no more expression than a statue. Disappointed, Hector sighed.

Romo leaned in close, his lips nearly touching Hector's ear.

"She needs the blood of another to make the blessings complete."

Hector jumped at the words but quickly nodded. *Of course she does*, he thought, gazing at her face again. It all made perfect sense.

He stared at her teeth, his heart yearning, desire bubbling for just one more smile, for just one more look of admiration, just one more tiny sign to show her promises of prosperity and happiness filling his mind moments ago were not empty but genuine. He searched her eyes, her expression, her mouth, her bony features. His eyes swept to her arms, her brightly colored clothing, her fingers, and then to the bowl of his own blood and back to her face. His mind screamed for recognition and he dug the nails of curved fingers into the palm of his hand, as if the pain would unleash more of her special favor, yet one more taste of her blessed regard. He was a loyal subject in search of his glorious leader. His quest was proving futile and his head began to droop in despair. A flutter of movement caught his attention, and he thrust his face upward so quickly that his neck kinked. Was it real? Was it imagined? In his mind, he saw clearly and he gasped.

His dear Lady had winked.

Heat coursed through Hector's body and his face took on an expression of sheer ecstasy, his eyes so wide the irises seemed like lost little dots among giant seas of white. He dared not blink or even breathe. The image was already fading from his mind, and as it edged into the shadows, he remained immobile, praying for a sign to show it wasn't just his imagination. It couldn't be, he thought. It had to be real. She graced him with her favor and Hector was captured by her spell. He wanted nothing more than to do her bidding.

Romo, chuckling, nodded with satisfaction at Juan, then disappeared into the back of the house.

Juan clasped Hector hard by his shoulder and pulled at him.

"Come on, Hector." Hector turned toward him with wet eyes. He nodded dumbly and stumbled to his feet. The air seemed warmer, the type of warm that lulled one into a nap, and Hector fought the urge to lay back on the floor. A loud caw broke his reverie and startled, he turned to see a small metal cage by the front door, inside of which perched a crow. It ruffled its feathers then hopped off its perch to the bottom of the cage, and began pecking furiously at something red. As Hector walked closer, he saw with surprise it was the blood-stained cloth from the bowl. Juan reached for the doorknob and pointed at the cage.

"Grab that. Romo wants you to take him."

HECTOR

Surprised, Hector paused, then bent to grasp the handle. The crow spun until its eyes were fixed on Hector's. It let loose a stream of caws that sounded to Hector more like laughter than natural bird sounds. The beady-black eyes blinked rapidly and the crow went silent. Hector gave one final look to his black-hooded friend, but her skeleton eyes stayed stubbornly fixed on space. He imagined what she was thinking, though, and he whispered to her as he gingerly picked up the cage.

"I'll watch over him for you, don't you worry," he said, closing the door without a sound behind him.

CHAPTER FOUR

Hector placed the cage carefully in the corner of his room, then pulled a wobbly wooden chair close and sank onto the seat. A bit of broken wood stabbed him on his hip, and he reached back angrily to yank it. He felt as it peeled back from the seat and then snapped off, and with a flick of his wrist, he tossed it across the floor. He rubbed his hip and stared with interest at the crow, its black eyes staring right back at his.

"What's your name, little fella?"

It reminded him of the great tail grackles he used to see with his father on their frequent walks and fishing trips, only smaller in size and not quite as dark in color. As if reading his thoughts, the crow hopped so its back was toward Hector, exposing tail feathers extending a couple inches past its body.

"But your feathers aren't as long, are they?" Hector smiled, recalling the ridiculously long tails of the grackles. As if in answer, the crow spun back around and resumed his staring. Hector scrunched his nose and reached out a tentative finger, poking it lightly through the slats of the cage to stroke its gleaming black side.

"Ow!" Hector pulled back and looked at the blood on his finger, where the crow pecked him. With a glare, Hector pushed hard at the cage, watching with satisfaction as

HECTOR

the crow lost its balance and banged against the metal. He nursed his finger, muttering expletives mixed with condemnations at the crow.

"Caw!"

Something about the glint in the bird's eyes made him forget his finger and as he peered close, then leaned in for an even closer look, he caught sight of an image that made him gasp. It was the gentle surf of the ocean by his boyhood home, the place where his parents took him weekly; the place where he would build castles and collect shells and look for dolphins; the place where he would picnic and play; the place where he was last happy. He watched as the waves rolled across the rocks and crashed onto the sand, spraying light mist into the air and leaving a trail of bubbly foam as they receded back into the blue. One after another after another they pushed onto the sand, at first rough, almost violent, an invisible hand thrusting them against stone and dirt and shell, then tamed and quiet as they returned home, like weary travelers softened by a too-long journey. Hector tasted salt and gulped hard. The water poured from the crow's eye, filling the cage, filling the floor, filling the room. The crash of waves deafened him so that he held his hands over his ears, trying to block out the sound. Wind whipped his face and hair and he shut his eyes tight to the grains of swirling sand, battering his skin. Then with a *whoosh*, all was whisked away: the water, the sand, the sounds, all pressed into a single funnel shooting back into the cage, into the crow's eye. For a few long seconds, it was just Hector and the crow, staring motionless at each other.

"Caw!"

Hector, with a thud, toppled to the floor.

❋ ❋ ❋

"Hector, come here, I want to show you something."

Hector looked up from the floor where he was stretched flat on his stomach, busily assembling the pieces of a puzzle into a beautiful street scene that included a towering background shot of the Eiffel Tower—and smiled. His father looked so proud and strong in his police uniform, the black cloth so crisp and formal, the white of the letters on his shirt so clean they almost glowed. Hector pulled himself into a sitting position and groaned as his foot mistakenly kicked apart the corner section, a particularly difficult collection of tiny pieces of various shades of green that had taken him a good half hour to form. He quickly pushed them back together and admired his work once more.

"Come on." His father's voice was quiet but stern, and Hector jumped to his feet.

"Where are we going?" His father said nothing but pointed to Hector's shoes by the front door. Hector had barely pulled them on and was hopping awkwardly to keep pace with his father, who was already descending the porch stairs and striding toward the car. With a final tug of his shoestrings, Hector pushed through the door and let it slam shut. The voice of his mother made him stop and turn. She was angry, and when she was angry, she spoke in her native tongue so rapidly the words shot like darts from her mouth.

"Gabriel Menendez!" At that, Hector's dad turned too. His eyes, wide in surprise, dropped to the ground as he made his way back to the porch.

"Earlina," he said soberly. "You know our rule."

Hector watched as his mother's eyes narrowed, then softened, and the corners of her lips quivered as she fought to keep them straight. Gabriel leaned in and kissed her forehead and beneath the angle of his father's chin, Hector saw his mother's smile. By the time his father tilted his

HECTOR

head back, though, her lips were once again tight. Hector chuckled to himself. Try as she might, she could never stay angry, but she would rather step in a bed of fire ants with bare feet than let on to that truth.

"English only, right?" Gabriel turned and nodded toward Hector, then gazed at his wife's eyes once again. "For his sake."

Earlina nodded and swatted Gabriel's shoulder.

"You cannot leave and not say nothing on me," she said slowly, her forehead drawn tight with creases so deep Hector could count them from the driveway.

"You're right," Gabriel said, ignoring her grammar and instead hugging her tightly. "I'm sorry."

Hector watched as his father leaned in and whispered something in her ear. It must have been humorous, because she started laughing out loud then smacked him again playfully on the shoulder. Her laughter grew louder as he grabbed her around the waist and lifted her high into the air, spinning her until her hair came loose from its ribbon. Hector sighed and shook his head, unaware of the wide smile springing to his lips. His parents, as long as he could remember, had always been like that; always demonstrative with their love; his father, gentle; his mother, happy; together, as a family, a tight circle. Hector had friends, but he often preferred the company of his father. It wasn't that his friends weren't fun; it was just that his father showed him so many interesting places, and taught him so many fascinating things that no matter what they were doing, Hector felt important, like he was the center of a very special universe. Fishing just wasn't the same with his friends as it was with his father.

"Come on, let's go." His father clapped him on the shoulder as he walked past and opened the car door. Hector shot a quick wave at his mother, who was all smiles now, blowing kisses; then he hopped in the seat next to his father. The engine started with a roar, and for the next twenty minutes Hector listened intently as his father spoke of his favorite topic—God.

"It's not enough to say you believe in God," his father was saying. "You have to behave as if you believe in God too."

Hector glanced out the window as landscape whizzed by, trees blending against sky as if smeared by the stroke of an artist's paintbrush. He nodded and turned back to his father.

"A lot of people—too many people—wear a cross around their neck or carry a Bible with them in their car and say, 'Look at me, I'm a Christian, I'm doing God's work'—then you see them walk right by a beggar on the street or stand quietly by and do nothing as a group of kids bully a boy or worse." He glanced at Hector with a dark look on his face. "Or go to church on Sunday morning, then beat their wife on Sunday night. Or go out drinking and carousing with their no-good friends Friday and Saturday nights and spend all the rent and food money and let their kids go hungry the rest of the week."

Hector stared curiously at his father's profile, a question on his lips.

"Yes," Gabriel said quietly, sadness in his tone, "before you ask, I do know people like that. Too many people like that." He paused and turned his face to the ground, speaking in so low a voice Hector had to strain to hear. "You see the worst of the worst in my line of work. Satan certainly rules this world."

They rode for some minutes in silence, the sound of the tires growing louder as Gabriel turned down a dirt road. Little rocks spit up against the windshield, leaving a chip

HECTOR

at the spot right in front of Hector's face. Hector watched as the crack caught a ray of sun and flashed brightly for a moment, then went dark. He squinted as hard as he could, trying to gauge the size of the chip, and as he was leaning forward for a better look, a row of tiny houses appeared just over the dash. He watched as they grew larger. The closer they approached, the bumpier the ride became until finally he couldn't keep the houses from bouncing from bottom to top of the windshield, and from left to right. His father, with a loud sigh, stopped the car.

"We'll walk from here," he said, opening his door then stretching a long arm into the backseat to grab something. Hector saw it was a black leather duffel bag, packed so tight the zipper strained and left a couple inches gap at the end. With a heave, Gabriel slung it over his shoulder and stepped from the car.

"Come on." He slammed the door hard and Hector hurried to follow.

"Are you going to arrest someone?" Hector struggled to catch his breath. He had to jog to keep up but at the same time, watch for the deep potholes in the road. His head was down and he didn't notice in time his father had spun to face him. Hector crashed into his chest and bounced back, his knee twisting painfully in the process.

"Arrest someone?" Gabriel looked puzzled, then looked down and ran a hand down his shirt collar, patting the name tag of his uniform as realization dawned. "No, Hector. No, I'm not going to arrest anyone." He smiled and ruffled Hector's hair.

"Come on. Let's go." Gabriel put an arm about Hector's shoulder and they walked that way for several steps, both taking care to avoid the holes, especially the ones brimming with dirty brown water.

CHERYL CHUMLEY

"I want you to pay attention to all you see in the next few minutes and never forget it."

Hector nodded, surprised, but intrigued. They drew closer to the homes, and the closer they got the less like houses they looked and the more like shanties. Hector scrunched his nose in disgust.

"What's that smell?" He put a hand over his face reflexively, breathing out hard as if to rid his nose of the odor. When that didn't work, he pinched his nostrils tight between his thumb and forefinger, and made gagging noises.

"Quiet, Hector." His father shot him a stern look and Hector immediately dropped his hand. He still held his breath, though, as long as he could, and when he couldn't hold it any longer, he exhaled then inhaled as lightly as possible, trying to avoid the taste of the foul air. He noticed a woman standing by her front door and wearing a torn flower-patterned dress watching them closely as they approached. She held a towel in one hand while the other was planted on the railing of her porch, a rickety piece of work that seemed to shed chips of paint in real time. When Hector first saw her, he guessed her to be in her twenties, but with each step, she aged. By the time he and his father arrived at her doorstep, she was in her forties and fading fast. The wrinkles on her face told of a life of worry, but the hardness of her eyes spoke of something deeper, something darker. They were brown, almost black, and they didn't gaze so much as pierce. Hector found himself unable to hold her stare and he glanced nervously about, wishing for some sort of safe landing point for his eyes that wouldn't offend her and draw even more scrutiny.

"*Hola, señora. ¿Cómo te va?*"

Hector looked with surprise at his father. He rarely spoke anything other than English and insisted on the family

HECTOR

doing the same. One of Hector's earliest memories was of his father telling of the time when they would all move to America for a new life. It was an oft-repeated story in their home, and perfecting English was part of the preparation.

The woman pursed her lips and gave only a short nod in reply. A sudden movement to the left of the house grabbed all their attention, and with a sharp cry, the woman threw down her towel and stomped off the porch.

The target of her frustration were two small children, a boy and a girl, both outfitted in nothing but diapers and T-shirts, the hems of which were too short to cover their pale bellies. The white of their skin against their bony ribs contrasted markedly with the dirty blackness of their bare feet. As Hector watched, the girl stumbled and toppled to the ground, spilling the contents of an orange bucket onto the leg of the other child in the process. Thick mud oozed down the boy's thigh and he let out a wail so loud, Hector winced. Before the woman could reach them, he stretched out a tiny arm and smacked his hand hard once, twice, several times against the girl's head. She shrieked in pain, and coddled her head in her arms, as the woman with one well-trained movement scooped both to her side, straightened their bodies to face the porch, then marched them quick-time to the house. Hector's mouth dropped open as he watched their filthy bodies pass by and disappear behind a screen door.

For several seconds, the discomforting sound of bawling children filled the air, then there was a sharp rap and all went quiet. Hector couldn't tell if the smack was the woman's hand striking a cheek or of her palm hitting hard against a table. But in the ensuing silence, he shifted nervously from one foot to the next and held his breath, praying to hear even the littlest sounds from at least one of the children. He looked to his father and saw his face stretched tight with anxiety as well. Just then, the door burst back open and the woman, once again holding her towel, stepped onto the porch and walked slowly toward them.

"Hector," his father said, in a voice barely above a whisper, "why don't you go get the bucket and see if you can rinse it with that hose over there." Hector followed his father's finger to the side of the house, a twisted mess of kinked hose attached to a spigot.

He glanced at the woman and nodded. Up close, her dress was even more ripped than he had first imagined, and the top of her bra clearly spilled from between a rip in the thin cloth. Hector, embarrassed, looked away. His mother would have a term for a woman who dressed so improperly, though he wasn't sure if she would have the same reaction in this particular situation, where he and his father intruded without notice. Either way, Hector's cheeks reddened and he stomped a bit as he walked away, angry at himself for showing his embarrassment. He picked up the bucket and shook it hard, sending the remainder of the mud to the ground with a satisfying thump.

From the corner of his eye, he watched his father lean in close and say something to the woman that must have been good news because her lips curved into a smile and while her face didn't exactly light with joy, it did seem to lose some of its wrinkles for a few seconds. Gabriel extended the black bag with both hands, then pulled back the zipper and watched as her head lowered for a look. She reached in with a tentative touch and gently sifted through the items. Hector strained to see the contents as he idly sprayed water into the bucket and absently shook it by the rim. He saw colored cloth, which he guessed were clothes, then he heard her gasp. As he watched, he let the nozzle drop to his side,

HECTOR

paying no attention to the flow of water dampening the house. In her hand was a stack of bills.

Even from across the yard, Hector could see it was a thick stack—more money than he had ever seen held by one hand in his entire life. The water sprayed against his shoes, soaking through the toes, and he quickly leaned over and flipped off the spigot. When he looked again, the money was gone and his father was zipping the bag and handing it to her. She reached two arms around Gabriel's neck and pulled tight. Hector walked slowly toward them, his mind racing with questions and his mouth in the shape of a perfect "O."

She flashed Hector a surprisingly pretty smile and he paused, mid-step.

"Your papa a saint," she said, her English stilted and broken.

Gabriel simply patted her shoulder and then dropped his head. Reaching for Hector's hand, he then looked expectedly at the woman. She hesitated, then with another smile, held out a palm. Hector grasped it, feeling bones so tiny he dared not clamp it tight, and Gabriel reached for her other, then lowered his head and shut his eyes.

"Dear Father, who art in heaven, hallowed be Thy name, Thy kingdom come, Thy will be done, on earth as it is in heaven. Please give us this day our daily bread and forgive us our sins, as we forgive those of our debtors and lead us not into temptation but deliver us from evil. In the name of Jesus Christ, Your Son, our glorious Savior, we pray. Amen," he said softly, opening his eyes again.

The woman's expression was somber and she stared intently at Gabriel, as if waiting for more.

"Jesus loves you," Gabriel said, dropping Hector's hand and taking both of the woman's in his own. "He loves you and will protect you and will save you if you take Him into your heart and confess your sins and accept that He died on the cross so that you might have eternal life with Him in heaven. Do you believe that? Do you know Jesus?"

The woman nodded, her eyes glistening and bright.

"Jesus. I know from little girl, from stories." She stopped, scrunching her nose as if searching for words.

"You know Jesus from stories you were told when you were a little girl?"

"Yes!" She smiled triumphantly at Gabriel, nodding several times. "Yes, Jesus. He come to church." She gave up the English and started chattering in her native language, pausing every few seconds to wait for Gabriel to nod. After several more minutes, and at least two more hugs, the woman stopped talking and looked right into Hector's eyes.

"He a saint," she proclaimed loudly, pointing to Gabriel while smiling broadly at Hector. "You be good boy. For him. For Jesus."

Gabriel turned before she could hug him again, leaving Hector the only one within her grasp. He stiffened as she pulled him close and he fought the urge to make a face. She smelled like sweat that hadn't been washed away for days, and there was something else—something sour wafting from her as she turned and rested her head against his shoulder. But he didn't want to be rude so he held his breath and gave her a quick hug. Finally, she stepped back and Hector seized the opportunity and hurried after his father.

He glanced for a final look and saw that even through brown-stained teeth, her smile was almost attractive. There was something endearing about the way she waved with one hand and clutched tight the bag to her chest with the other, like a little girl delighted by a Christmas gift. Hector, his heart suddenly jumping, raised his hand in the air, fingers

HECTOR

stretched straight, a final goodbye. Her smile grew wider and she waved even more enthusiastically.

Hector turned and looked at his father's face. For one shocking second, he thought he saw a patch of wetness in the corner of his eye. Then the light shifted and Gabriel moved his head and the wetness was gone. Hector, still staring, decided he must have imagined it.

"She had been saved when she was a little girl," Gabriel said, holding open the car door for Hector and waiting until he climbed onto the seat. He shut it with a bang then walked to his side and slipped behind the steering wheel. "But she had a hard life. Her parents died when she was still a girl and she married young so she wouldn't have to go to the orphanage. But her husband was cruel. He beat her and left her with two babies. She's been on her own for two years now, trying to find work and feed her children." Gabriel swung the car around and navigated carefully along the road, swerving gently to avoid the potholes. He glanced at Hector and sighed.

"She thought Jesus forgot all about her. She thought Jesus stopped loving her." His voice cracked and Hector looked at him sharply. Gabriel cleared his throat hard. "But Jesus never stops loving His children and never forgets them either."

They rode in silence for several minutes, and Hector squinted his eyes tight, trying to imagine what it would be like to be one of those dirty children. He wondered what they ate, what kind of food they had for breakfast, what their bedrooms looked like—if they even had their own bedrooms, which he doubted as he then thought of the size of the square broken box they called home. He bit his bottom lip distractedly, feeling shame now at his disgust at the woman's sour smell as he tried to picture what her laundry room looked like. He then realized she probably didn't have one—she probably had to cart her dirty clothes, along with her dirty kids, to a place where they had laundry machines, and then pay to use them. He didn't remember seeing a car in her yard. He tried to imagine how it would be to sit there for hours in a laundry place, with two bored children and probably nothing to eat and no money to buy anything to drink, and just wait and wait and wait for the machines to finish. Unconsciously, he sighed. He probably would have stinky clothes too, he decided.

"What's the matter, son?"

Startled, Hector looked up. He hadn't realized he had been shaking his head back and forth. He stumbled to speak, overwhelmed by the stark contrasts he was realizing between his life and that of the woman's and her children. Inexplicably, a sob rose in his throat and he choked hard to stifle it.

Gabriel reached over and gave him a reassuring pat on the shoulder.

"Do you know why I go there in my uniform, Hector?"

Hector shook his head slightly, not trusting himself to talk.

"I go there in my uniform because I want them to see not all police are bad, police can be trusted, there are police who aren't corrupted by the cartels and—and this is most important—God uses police for His purposes. I want them to see police in a good way, in a godly way, in a way that lets them believe in justice and law and order, and to know it does exist." He paused, letting his words sink in, then glancing to see if Hector understood before finishing.

"I want them to know some police aren't afraid of the evil," he said. "And I want the evil to know that too."

Hector smiled, his eyes filling with admiration and understanding as he stared at his father's profile.

HECTOR

"What did you give her?" Hector finally asked, thinking of the stack of bills she had pulled from the bag.

His father shot him a look then reached over and ruffled his hair.

"It's not the amount that matters. It's what's in here," he said, thumping his chest with one fist, then spreading his fingers so the thumps turned into pats.

Gabriel steered into their driveway, flicked off the ignition key, then turned so he was facing Hector. His eyes were dark and serious and Hector sat a little straighter, waiting for the bit of life lesson he knew was coming. He loved when his father spoke to him in that deep, soft voice, imparting wisdoms, explaining mysteries, clarifying the correct path to take. Somewhere in the back of his mind, he knew there would come a day when maybe he'd resent his father for speaking in such manner, for taking it on himself to tell him how to act or what to do or whether or not he should or shouldn't; subconsciously he knew he'd reach an age where he perhaps wouldn't want his father to tell him things because he would rather decide himself. But now, in the car, facing the dark eyes, and with the memory of the woman and her children and their tragic poverty fresh in his mind, Hector waited with warm anticipation for his father to speak.

Gabriel leaned toward Hector, his mouth open to speak, when his eyes rolled upward and he gazed with intensity at something out the window. Hector saw the lines on his father's forehead and turned first left, then right, trying to see the distraction. Gabriel muttered to himself and tore out the car door. Hector, confused, followed. His father raced past him so quickly Hector, for the second time that day, almost fell. In the street were parked three luxury sedans, all black, all with tinted windows. Hector took in the sight as he mounted the front steps behind his father, who stopped with his hand on the door knob. The door was cracked open, the soft light of the foyer poking like a slit between the frame and dark mahogany, and Gabriel paused, with Hector behind him, neither letting go a breath. Finally, Gabriel pushed gently, letting the door drift open an inch at a time, his knuckles clenched tight on the handle, his face drawn in a tense frown. From behind the bulk of his father, Hector caught sight of a hand. It was lying on the floor, palm upward, fingers crooked and dangling, protruding from a limp wrist jutting strangely from the bottom corner of the kitchen island. The golden ring and bronze-colored fingertips were unmistakable. He sucked in hard and gasped, at the same time his father rushed forward, a single word shouting from his lips.

"Earlina!"

Hector stopped at the doorway in horror as his father sank to his knees and bent low, grabbing his mother's hand while scooting close to her body, the rest of his activities obscured by the cabinet. He couldn't see his father's face but heard the panicked cry.

"Earlina! Dear God, Earlina!"

A sudden flurry to his right made Hector involuntarily duck, and when he raised his head, he was shocked to see a band of men moving too quickly to count, attacking his father, kicking him, cursing him, punching at his body. Hector's mouth opened wide to shout, but in terror, nothing came out and then he felt his vision go watery and it was as if he were floating. He couldn't feel his feet, he couldn't feel his hands, he couldn't feel his heartbeat, but it was as if he were fighting to keep from being sucked into a dark unseen tunnel pulling from behind him.

HECTOR

Then he saw the men drag his father from behind the counter into full view and it was as if he were suspended in time, forced to watch the beating, forced to witness the blood flying from places unknown. He saw through the blur the dark eyes of his father and they fixed on his and for a moment, time stopped; a father gazing in compassion at a frightened son. Then the dark eyes blinked and Hector watched in horror as his father tried futilely to shield his face from his attackers. A loud bang sounded, then another, and Hector let loose a scream. He fell onto the body that was his mother's, grasping desperately at shoulders. But she didn't move.

"Mama!"

Then another bang sounded and he saw through his tears five bronze-tipped fingers fall flat onto the floor. He struggled against the strong arms that suddenly held him to see his mother's face, to rush to help his father to his feet, to stop the men from carting him from his home. But it was of no use. Hector was carried to one of the three black sedans he saw parked in the street and roughly shoved into the back seat. Before he could reach the door handle, two oversize bodies shoved next to him, one on each side. Hector heard a squeal of tires, and then his head was thrown against the back of the seat. He glanced at the dark unshaven face of the man to his right and swallowed hard at the two black eyes returning his look. The man snarled and turned a steel black barrel toward Hector's chest.

"You got a new family now, hombre."

Hector felt his insides turn cold. He didn't think it so much as felt it, but his days of carefree youthfulness had just come to an end.

CHAPTER FIVE

With a gasp, Hector opened his eyes and sucked hard, like a drowning man whose lungs were suddenly pumped with air.

"Caw! Caw!"

Confused, still choking, he grappled on the floor to sit up and turned toward the sound of the bird. There sat the crow, just inches from Hector's face, its black eyes gleaming and unblinking. The unlatched door of its cage gently clicked against metal, bouncing slightly once, twice, then settling in a half-open state. Hector looked from the cage to the bird, then back to the cage again. He shuddered as much from the vivid images from his dream as from his certainty the cage door had been locked.

The crow fluttered his wings and hopped closer to Hector's face. Instinctively, he thrust his arm at the bird, pushing with such force it let loose a stream of raucous protests. Hector sat up and wiped the sweat from his forehead, then looked at his fingers. They were drenched. He glanced at the alarm clock on his bedside table, then at the window with its blackened glass. Juan didn't let any of his charges, his "esclavos," as he mockingly called them, stay in rooms with windows that weren't completely darkened with paint. He said it was so nobody could see in, but Hector thought it was so nobody could see out too—so nobody under Juan's

HECTOR

control could gaze out the window and imagine a life outside the cartel. Imagining, after all, might lead to fleeing.

Hector lay an open palm against his heart, feeling its racing beat. The dream had been so real his body was pumping adrenaline. He took several deep breaths, trying to calm himself before Gio came to get him, as every night at this time. He had about a half hour. He decided to forgo the shower, and instead, curled his legs under his chin and dropped his head on his knees, shutting his eyes tight as if blocking out something painful.

It wasn't a horrible life, all things considered, he told himself. He had learned over the years that if he repeated it enough times, his stomach would stop hurting and his head would stop spinning and that little clump of nausea that always formed in the pit of his throat each evening, as the hour drew close, would dry up and disappear.

What never disappeared, though, were the dreams of the brown-haired girl with smoky gray eyes. She had been his overdose victim, and nearly two years later, nearly two years after her death, her pale face still darted into his dreams and the memory of her cold fingers and lifeless body as he tried desperately to shake her awake still gave him shivers. Her name was Willow.

Hector sucked at air to slow his heart, then squeezed his eyes tight and groaned, helpless to stop his thoughts from taking him back to that night. The memories were so vivid it was almost as if Gio were right in the room with him, chortling triumphantly about the girl he predicted to become their next addicted customer. Hector's breathing quickened and for a second, he even thought he smelled cigarette smoke. That was all it took and from there, the memories flooded, and he dug his nails deep into his palms. Another flashback, another torrent of guilt at what he had

CHERYL CHUMLEY

done—at what the turn of events since his parents' murder brought him to do.

. . .

"She's gonna be a regular," Gio said with a hoot, pulling a wad of bills from his pocket and flapping them against Hector's face to drive home his point. Hector flicked away Gio's hand and flashed him an angry look. He raised his hand to flip him the middle finger but stopped halfway, before deciding against it and dropping his arm back to his side. In the weeks they had worked the street together, Gio had only lost his temper twice, and neither time at Hector. But Hector cringed at the thought of one of Gio's victims, remembering the tiny sound the guy's teeth made as they clattered onto the sidewalk. In the right light, the blood stain was still visible, a tiny set of black and crimson dots right at the curb. Hector glanced sidewise at Gio and shrugged. That guy may have deserved it; high and reckless, he had tried to rob Gio of his stash. But why tempt fate, Hector thought. He watched as Gio separated large bills from small and put the ones and fives back into his pocket. The others he shoved into the toe of his sock then jammed his foot back into his sneaker. Gio grinned and tapped his foot firmly.

"Ain't nobody taking me for a ride," he said with a snort.

"How do you know?" Hector waited for Gio to answer and when he didn't, he asked again. "How do you know she's a regular?"

Gio looked past Hector to the girl with long straight brown hair who had just handed them a clump of bills.

"I just know, is all," Gio said. He spun to face Hector. "Look, they're all the same. They come by for a bump, for a single, for just something to get them through the night. We give 'em the good stuff, so they get good and high. Then next time they need something, they remember how

HECTOR

good the stuff was we gave 'em so they come hunting for us. After a few times, we stop giving the good stuff—but by then they don't just want it, they need it. So they're gonna pay more to get more so they can get the same high. They just don't know that we're giving them weak on purpose so they gotta spend more." He let out a long, hard laugh that went on for several seconds and only ended when he started choking.

"And that girl? That Willow?" Gio coughed to clear his throat. "She been here five, six times already in the last couple weeks. She about ready to drop some money." He emphasized the last couple words, drawing out "money" so it sounded more like "Muhh-nee."

Hector watched as she turned the corner and disappeared from view. He knew where she was going next. Around that corner was Leon, waiting with the small plastic baggie she had just purchased. For a moment, he thought of running after her, grabbing her by the arm, shaking her and screaming into her face, "Go home! Go home to your mother!"—an impulse made all the stronger by the face of his own mother as she lay dying on the kitchen floor. Then he looked at the dirt on the broken-down cars parked by the curb and at the graffiti painted on the boarded-up windows of the closed shops lining the street, and then at Gio, haphazardly balancing a half-rolled marijuana joint in one palm as he worked busily to pinch it into shape and light it, and Hector cleared his throat and shook his head, remembering where he was—remembering what his life had become. There was no sense crying about it. He swallowed and clenched his teeth hard. That girl would have to figure it out on her own, he decided.

"They're all the same," Gio said, sucking deeply then holding out the joint to Hector. Hector paused, then gave a quick shake of his head. He had yet to try any of the product they sold, but with each passing day, with each evening's work, with each exhausted drop into fitful sleep behind windows painted black, he could feel his will weakening and his temptation growing.

He wondered at the day he would break. He wondered if it would come as an overwhelming desire, the final caving to tortured whispers that could no longer be ignored or disobeyed, and if so, whether his submission would be soft and gentle or tainted with anger and self-loathing; or if the end would come much more suddenly, as a force so powerful from an event so dramatic only a mind-numbing drug could conceal the pain.

He wondered when that day would come and imagined its events.

He didn't wonder whether that day would come.

"Yeah, they're all the same," Gio repeated, flashing Hector a dark look and finishing off the joint himself. Hector pretended not to see Gio's disapproval. He knew every time he refused a hit, Gio took it as a personal affront. Hector bit his lip and beckoned with his chin toward the street. Willow was walking slowly toward them, her head down, her hands jammed in the side pockets of her denim jacket. Her brown hair blew wildly in the breeze, but she didn't bother brushing it off her face. Hector saw as she drew closer how strands were stuck into the sides of her mouth and when she spoke, they formed tight little lines across her cheek. He stared at them and fought the urge to flick them from her face.

"Yeah? Whatchyou need, baby girl?" Gio sauntered toward her, his chest out, chin high. His voice boomed in the abandoned streets and Willow took a startled step backward, letting her hands drop from her pockets. She

HECTOR

swept her eyes across Gio's face, then flitted them to Hector. With a gasp, Hector saw two huge pools of silky gray staring at him. For a moment, her face seemed lit by a ray of sun, whisps of her hair burning like golden embers around her cheeks. Then she dropped her eyes and muttered something and Hector realized it was actually dusk and the sun was hidden. He smirked at his own stupidity.

"Come on now, don't be shy." Gio reached forward and rubbed her arm, grinning widely and stepping closer. "Tell Gio what you need."

Without a word, Willow thrust a fist into her jacket pocket and pulled out a mass of bills. She held them out and tilted her head almost shyly as she looked sidewise at Gio's face. Gio burst out laughing, his voice mocking and sarcastic.

"What'd you do to get that, baby girl?"

Willow stood with her head down, waiting motionless for Gio to take the bills. Gio regarded her for a few seconds then shot Hector a bemused smile.

"I know what you did," he sang softly, whistling through his teeth. Hector strained to catch a glimpse of Willow's expression, but her hair hung on both sides of her bent head, hiding her face.

With a quick motion, Gio grabbed the money and stepped back onto the curb.

"Told ya, man," he said, biting his words and snickering. "Told ya. They're all the same." He waited for her reaction, and when there was none, he shot his arm toward her face, his fingers extended, not caring if they grazed her nose.

"Go on." Gio's voice was nearly a shout. "Get off with ya." Gio turned back to his money, counting bills and separating the ones for his pocket from the ones for his sock. Hector watched as she headed back to the familiar corner once again, sadness creeping into his heart. She was such a little thing, he thought. All bones, all pale skin. He wondered at the evils those gray eyes had seen; at the dark events they had watched unfold; and he wondered at what point those gray eyes had seen enough that they had to be consoled with drugs.

He wondered at what point his own would have to be consoled.

"Ahlright, we good for tonight." Gio smacked his hands together so loudly Hector jumped. "We made our quota. Let's cut out early and slip by Teresa's."

Teresa was famous on the streets for late-night concessions. Hector didn't want to go, but he had already turned down Gio once that evening. He didn't dare do it again. With a sigh so quiet he knew Gio didn't hear, Hector nodded.

"Okay."

They headed in the same direction as Willow, turning the corner and giving a slight wave to Leon as they passed the window of the abandoned building where he sat.

"Going to T's, man. Wanna come?"

They waited until Leon popped out the doorway.

"We made bank?" He smiled when Gio pulled forth a huge wad of cash and nodded vigorously.

"That's just the small stuff," Gio said, stuffing it back in his pocket. "The rest hidden away." He pointed at his shoe.

Leon broke into a grin and smacked Gio on the back, then Hector, even harder.

"Hector finally gonna get him some, huh?"

Hector gave a weak smile. But his eyes were trained at a spot about fifty yards away and he squinted in the dim streetlights to make out what it was. Something about the hump spilling off the curb and into the street seemed familiar. He was just about to tap Gio on the shoulder to ask him what he thought when all of a sudden, realization

HECTOR

struck and his eyes widened in terror. With a gasp, he took off running.

"What the—" Leon's surprised shout called to him as he ran but Hector didn't bother to turn. The closer his steps took him to the lump in the road the more his panic grew. The color of her jacket came into focus and then there was no mistaking the cascade of brown hair that spilled onto her face, into the dirty water where the street met the curb. He raced to her side and dropped to his knees, ignoring for the moment the needle that fell from her hand as he cradled her head. The skin on her face was an unnerving shade of blue and her lips were almost purple. He felt her wrist for a beat, then in desperation, placed his fingers alongside her neck, a couple inches from the ear. He waited for what seemed like minutes. But there was nothing there. His hands fell limply by his side and he sat gazing at her dead face, transfixed by the coldness of her unblinking eyes that looked up from his lap. They were dark gray, much darker than he remembered, and as he stared in horror and helplessness, a single, fearful thought crept into his mind, and he felt its truth as if struck like a bullet.

I did this, he thought.

I did this.

With a cry, he twisted his body to the side and her head struck pavement with a smack. Hector gagged then vomited, then vomited again, until his stomach had nothing left to give. He didn't notice Leon and Gio by his side but felt a hand on his shoulder and looked up in surprise.

"Gotta go, Hector! Gotta go! Let's go."

Hector heard the words from a distance, as if someone were shouting down a long tunnel and the voice was echoing and bouncing so much the message was indecipherable. He felt his body jerk and then somehow, his legs were moving, stumbling foot over foot, toe over heel, and he knew he was just about to smash his face on the street, but then something gripped his shoulder tight and he called out in pain.

"Come on, Hector! Run!"

Hector obeyed, his mind turning in confusion and his eyes closing then opening, then sweeping chaotically from building to ground to sky to ground again. He struggled to breath and a rancid taste in his mouth nearly made him vomit again. But the force on his arm wouldn't let him stop. Minutes passed into days or so it seemed, then Hector felt his body thrown sidewise into something soft. He felt cloth and metal and opened his eyes to see a large windshield inches from his face. He heard an engine start then tires peeling on wet road. He looked to his left and saw Leon, behind the wheel of their truck. He looked to his right and saw Gio, staring expressionless out the front window. He waited for someone to say something, to make sense of what had just happened, to maybe explain why and how and what was next and what would happen to Willow. Nobody said a word. They arrived at home and parked in silence. Hector stared soundlessly at Juan's house and for once, the sight of the black painted windows didn't make his stomach clench with anxiety. He felt nothing, in fact.

He felt completely numb.

But her eyes stayed with him, and he went to sleep that night, and every night thereafter, trying to imagine what was behind the veil of smoky gray . . .

His bedroom door flew open, snapping Hector awake and sending the crow fluttering into the corner of the room.

"Wake up, homie! Time to go to work." Gio didn't wait for a response but for emphasis, smashed the door into the wall then strode down the hallway.

HECTOR

"Caw!"

Hector sat up slowly and turned toward the crow. With a fright, he saw two smoky gray eyes staring back at him.

"Skinny Lady, help me!" The prayer burst from Hector's lips and the image suddenly flooding his mind of a skeletal figure wearing a dark hood and eye sockets glowing fiery red frightened him almost as much as the crow's unnatural eyes. The hair on his arms stood up straight and he crouched, his head in his hands, his fingers rubbing hard on his temples.

"Caw!"

When he lifted his head to look, its eyes were glassy black again.

CHAPTER SIX

Hector stumbled down the dark hallway, tripping over his boots as he rushed to the door. The honking of the truck's horn was growing angrier and Hector fought to clear his mind of the images of the past few minutes and shift focus to the night's work. Gio would be ticked off and impatient, and that was never a good start to the evening.

He could see through the windshield Gio's mouth moving at a rapid pace, and as he approached the passenger door, he caught several colorful phrases thrown his way, but Hector pretended not to hear as he jumped in his seat. Almost immediately, Gio spun the truck wheels into reverse and sped down the road, his words growing quieter as he drove, as if he were mumbling to himself. Hector kept his eyes fixed out the window, waiting for Gio to finish.

"You have a special job tonight, homey."

Hector turned and looked at Gio's profile but said nothing. Gio, meanwhile, pulled out a pack of cigarettes from inside his jacket, dug in deep to his jeans pocket and with difficulty, produced a light blue lighter. He moved slowly, deliberately, enjoying the drama of letting his words hang in the air as he flicked the flame at the tip of his cigarette and sucked hard. Slowly, he let the smoke flow from his mouth, then cupped his lips expertly in a circle and blew. He smiled at the rings and blew two more. He glanced at

HECTOR

Hector and frowned. Hector was staring out the window again, his face glum, his mouth unmoving.

"Yep. It's straight from Juan," Gio said, this time blowing smoke across the seat so it drifted to Hector's window. He tapped with frustration on the steering wheel. Hector's silence was growing uncomfortable, and Gio rolled down his window to toss out his cigarette butt, then immediately lit another.

"Hey." Gio reached over with his right arm and flicked the back of his hand hard at Hector's chest. Hector looked in the direction of Gio's pointed finger.

"Let's make a quick stop." Gio steered into a parking space and rammed the shifter into park. "Trust me," he said, leaning toward Hector at the same time opening his driver door, "you're gonna want this tonight." Hector furrowed his brows at Gio's conspiratorial tone. He hesitated, reading the storefront sign, all lit in bright red letters: "ALCOHOL." Gio smacked him again.

"Let's go."

Hector's mind flashed on the hushed conversation he overheard between Juan and Leon, and the hair on his arms stood on end at the sudden thought.

"Hey, where's Leon tonight?" Hector held his breath, unsure if he wanted the answer.

Gio shrugged and yanked at the store door.

"Oh, he'll meet us later." He strode toward the back, where the coolers were located.

Hector followed, an odd feeling in the pit of his stomach. It wasn't usual for Leon to let them head out alone, without at least first giving them their quotas as well as their warnings about what would befall if they failed to meet them. As a matter of fact, Hector could only think of two occasions when Leon wasn't on hand for the start of their night's work and both times were because of Juan. One time, Juan showed up unannounced and took Leon somewhere else; where, Hector hadn't known and hadn't dared to ask.

"Meet us? Meet us where?" Hector grabbed hurriedly at the two separate six packs of beer Gio thrust into his arms. Holding a six-pack himself, Gio marched toward the counter, not bothering to answer Hector. Hector waited until they paid and were back in the truck.

"So where's he meeting us?"

Gio popped open a beer can and took a long drink. He beckoned to the six packs on the seat between them.

"Drink."

Hector slowly opened his can and sipped, feeling the pit grow deeper in his stomach and swallowing with difficulty. They rode in silence, Gio gulping while Hector sipped. After his fourth, Gio tossed his can on the floor and glanced down at the remaining cans of unopened beer on the seat.

"Drink up, amigo. That's your liquid courage tonight. You gonna need every bit of it."

Hector took another sip. His can was still nearly full and he was having trouble swallowing over the lump in the back of his throat. He shifted and something sharp stuck his thigh. Reaching down with his right hand, he dug into his pocket and felt the pointed edge of the cross, then the smooth circles of chain. It felt warm in his fingers and he stroked it lightly as he took another drink. He had forgotten it was in his pocket and he was about to pull it out and place it around his neck when a searing pain ripped through his head, like someone had poured a hot liquid on his brain, and the skeletal face of the Skinny Lady flashed right before him. Her eyes glowed ominously—it was as if they pierced right into his head, ripping apart the cross.

HECTOR

He let his fingers open wide and pulled them from his pocket. The pain immediately stopped and almost without knowing, he held his breath. He reached up with one tentative finger and touched the back of his head, where the stabbing had hit hardest. He rubbed gently at first, then with more vigor as he realized the pain was really gone. A flood of exuberance rushed through his body and with a shout of glee, he guzzled the rest of his beer, tossed the can out the window and reached for another.

He flipped the tab and with a smooth, quick motion, lifted the can in toast to the missing passenger, the one who had saved him from his pain. He finished his beer in one long draft.

"What's up with you, bro." Gio shot him a look of scorn.

Hector laughed maniacally and threw his emptied can at the dash. He wasn't much of a drinker and the beer in combination with his nerves was making him jittery. The can bounced off the windshield and onto Gio's lap, striking him in the shoulder first. Gio reached across and smacked Hector's head.

"Chill out." He flashed a warning look at Hector and lit another cigarette. Impulsively, he held it out to Hector. His eyes widened in surprise when Hector grabbed it and stuck it between his lips, dragging expertly and then pursing and blowing.

"Look at that." Hector laughed loudly at the smoke rings drifting toward the dash, bringing on another strange look from Gio. Hector giggled as he said, in a sing-song voice, "Don't drink, don't smoke, what do ya do?" He turned toward Gio with a lopsided smile.

"Guess I do now," Hector chuckled, with a triumphant tone.

Gio opened his mouth to speak, but a loud horn drew his attention back to the road. He slammed on the brakes and let loose a string of curse words, then for added emphasis stuck two middle fingers out his window at the speeding car. Hector quickly stuck out his middle fingers too, totally unconcerned that Gio had just run the red light and almost killed them both.

"Let's chase 'em, Gio!" he shouted. "Can I get another smoke?" He didn't wait for reply but grabbed the pack from the seat and popped one between his lips. "Light, man. Gimme a light."

"Man, that beer just cut you wild, didn't it." Gio mumbled but smiled broadly, handing Hector the lighter and peeling across the intersection. He pulled out a bag of small blue tablets from his pocket and tossed a couple in his mouth.

"Gimme one." Hector held out his palm. Ignoring Gio's look of surprise, Hector dug into the bag and took two. Then he grabbed another beer, popped the tab and guzzled noisily.

"One now," he said, pinching the pill between his finger and thumb, and holding it dramatically for Gio to see. He tossed it into his mouth and took a long swig of his beer. Then he snickered and held the second pill for Gio to see, before placing it in his mouth and following it with a deep drink of his beer. "And the other one now." He burst out laughing at his joke and turned to his window, sticking his head out to catch the wind as Gio drove.

"We here, man." Gio pulled up to the curb on a street unfamiliar to Hector, and slowed until the truck drifted to a stop. He put a finger to his lips and said softly, "Ya gotta be real quiet now."

HECTOR

"Shhh," Hector giggled, mimicking Gio and putting his own finger to his mouth. He scratched himself in the process. "Ow!" Hector rubbed at his nose.

"Shut up!" Gio hissed and flicked him with the back of his hand on his shoulder. "Shut the hell up, man. You gonna get us killed."

The streets were dark, except for a single yellow street lamp casting an almost eerie shadow on the pavement that resembled a freakishly tall, thin figure. Hector stared at the shadow, mesmerized by its gauntness and its likeness to his Skinny Lady. Her eyes bore into his mind and he shuddered, remembering the fiery poker on his brain from just a few minutes ago. He started to reach for the cross in his pocket to throw it away but then thought better of it and put his hand tightly under his thigh. He was afraid to touch it even for a second. He hoped his Lady would understand.

"Hey." When Hector didn't respond, Gio slapped his shoulder. "Bro."

Hector turned slowly, still mesmerized, and his eyes fell on Gio's open palm. The silvery glint of the barrel shot captivating sparks into the air and Hector's mouth fell open as he watched them dance. It took a minute for his mind to register that the object in Gio's hand was a gun, but even then, his fear quickly faded and it was more seductress than siren and Hector couldn't help himself. He reached out a long, pointed finger to stroke its shiny metal. Back and forth and back again, he gently rubbed the smooth steel until, without realizing, its barrel was in his whole hand, his fingers tightly curved around the handle, and he was lifting it and turning it in the dim light through the windshield, as if scrutinizing a fine piece of jewelry, a diamond or rare gem, perhaps.

"What'd you say?" Gio's voice broke through his dream-like state and with a start, he shook his head. The Skinny Lady's whispers stopped, and Hector's eyes shot wide with surprise. He stared at the gun in disbelief. He hadn't even realized she had been whispering to him until his mind went dark with silence.

"I—I ..." Hector struggled to speak, unsure what to say.

"You said some gibberish, man. What'd you say?"

Hector could only stare blankly at Gio, and he fingered the gun absently, its metal cold in his hand now. He felt slightly nauseous, and wished the Skinny Lady would speak to him again. Her whispers were so comforting, so enchanting.

Gio shrugged.

"You losing it, man." He nodded in the direction of the building to their right. "See that house?"

Hector nodded dumbly, his tongue thick in his mouth and bile rising in his throat. He squeezed the gun hard in his hand, as if doing so would keep him from vomiting.

"You got a job to do tonight." Gio's voice was low, but with a tone of seriousness that made Hector's face spin toward him.

"There's a guy in there been stealing from Juan. You gotta take care of him."

Hector sucked in his breath sharply, but before he could say anything, the Skinny Lady's eyes were upon him, boring in deeply and darkly, hypnotizing him, captivating him, drawing him close. Without realizing, his one finger slipped from the handle onto the trigger and he sat there, staring at those shiny dots of coal, stroking the small metal tongue, feeling its rounded edges and wanting nothing more than to please his great Lady. From a distance, he heard a voice,

HECTOR

but it was muffled and besides, it was distracting him from those beautiful black eyes.

"Hector!"

Hector jolted at the sudden pain in his chest.

"Ow!" He rubbed at his front and cursed. "What'd you do that for?"

"What the hell, man. You were pointing the gun right at my head." Gio lit a cigarette and blew angry smoke at Hector's face. "You were pointing it right at my head," he said again. "What the hell's wrong with you? I was shouting at you." He let his voice trail as he blew smoke again. Hector sat in shocked silence, unsure how to respond. He looked at the gun in his hand, still grasped tightly, and dimly, as if recalling a dream on the cusp of disappearing, he saw his arm held out straight, gun steady, barrel just inches from Gio's face. He gasped.

He knew it had happened.

Gio suddenly stopped cursing and ducked his head beneath the steering wheel. He yanked at Hector's arm and pulled him down, so their faces were nearly touching on the seat.

"That's him. That's your guy." Gio's breath was hot and smelled of stale beer.

Hector's heart pumped hard and he lifted his head slowly, until just his eyes peered over the top of the dash. He squinted at the figures by the streetlamp. One was wearing a dark sweatshirt and black pants; another, a red hoodie with the top tied tight around his face so only his nose and mouth were visible; the third, a ball cap and some sort of baggy pants and matching shirt with a big number 12 in white on the back. They were standing in a tight circle, looking down at something in the hand of the red hoodie guy. Hector thought it was a cell phone, but he couldn't be sure.

CHERYL CHUMLEY

"Which one?" Hector dropped his head back onto the seat and waited for Gio to peek.

"Guy in dark shirt, nothing on his head."

Hector nodded, then stole a longer look, taking in his height, his frame size, his age. He was the tallest of the three, but the thinnest too. Hector figured if it came to it, he could take him. He watched as the red hoodie guy shoved whatever was in his hand back into his pocket, and then gave what seemed to be directions to the other two. The red hoodie guy then walked down the street and disappeared into the dark. After a moment, Ball Cap crossed the road and took up a spot on some front step stairs of someone's apartment. His figure blended into the shadows and Hector turned his attention back to Dark Shirt.

"Come on, man. Ya gotta get this done." Gio slipped his head up for another look then slouched back behind the wheel, his head dropped low into his shoulders. When Hector hesitated, Gio poked him on the shoulder. "You got no choice. Juan says."

Hector reached for another beer and as he drank, held out his empty hand, palm up, fingers spread wide.

"Gimme another one of those pills."

Gio dug into his pocket, pulled the bag forth and shook a single pill into Hector's hand. Hector swallowed it and sucked hard at the rest of his beer. He threw the can on the floor and with a dramatic wipe of his hand across his mouth, held out his hand again to Gio. Without a word, Gio placed the gun in his hand.

"It's full load."

Hector shoved it into the waistband in the back of his pants and, with an odd chuckle brimming with the kind of bravado only drugs and alcohol can bring, pushed open his door and dropped lightly to the ground. Dark Shirt's back

HECTOR

was to him and Hector kept his hands thrust deep in his pockets as he walked, his fingers nervously pressed firmly upon the pointy sides of the cross. A shadow flickered from somewhere to his left, but just as he was about to jerk his gaze that way, Dark Shirt spun around and Hector's eyes narrowed and he reached to the back of his pants for his gun. A loud bang sounded and for a second, Hector wondered if he had mistakenly fired his gun. He was reaching to his waistband to check when he heard another bang and instinctively, he ducked his head as he turned toward the sound.

Ball Cap was standing beside the driver's side of the truck, his arm held out long and straight so his hand was inches from the window, and in his hand he held a gun, its dark black metal stark in the street light. A third bang sounded and Gio's head seemed to jolt to the side. Dark splotches shot forth onto the windshield, and Hector's heart thudded hard in his chest.

Hector felt his body turn ice cold and he was dimly aware of the strain on the sides of his lips as he opened them wide in a scream, but the only sound that spewed forth was a strange, hoarse croak. He fought to swallow against his tightening throat and as Ball Cap ran from the truck—his legs chopping back and forth, back and forth, white flashes of canvas accompanied by a backdrop of eerie silence— Hector thought of old black and white movies, where the actors moved in slight jerky fashion and the sound from the screen was muffled, piped from another world.

Then Ball Cap reached the corner and disappeared from view and Hector was back in this world, hunkered on the ground, his knees boring deeply into concrete, his fingers aching from the metal of the gun's handle he squeezed too tightly. Dark Shirt!

Hector whipped around, his arm flailing wildly, ready to fire. But his mark had fled. Dark Shirt was nowhere to be seen.

Hector was alone on the street, and his mind reeled at the realization that Gio was almost certainly dead, and if so, that meant he was alone with a dead body. Panic took ahold as he stared at the truck. He could see Gio's head, what was left of it, leaning uncomfortably against his right shoulder. He stared, and the longer he stared, the more his terror grew, until finally, through the blood of the glass, he thought he saw two bloody lips stretched into a grotesque smile.

He gasped, unsure if his mind was playing tricks.

The sound of his voice in the street was enough to shake him to action. Hector stood and with smooth, deliberate motions, bent and laid the gun very carefully on the ground. Then, as if trying not to awaken someone, he stepped very quietly, very slowly away from it, never taking his eyes off the barrel. After a few feet was put between him and the gun, he turned and without looking to his left or to his right, sprinted as fast as he could in the opposite direction of the truck. It was only as he was running he thought of Dark Shirt and his friends. Gasping for breath, he ducked down street after street, dodging directions and switching from side to side, hoping his haphazard path would throw Gio's murderers off his track. Hector had no idea where the streets led, but he ran until he couldn't run any more. He ran until the city streets opened onto an empty lot and seeing bushes lining the far end of the lot, he made his way there and dove among the branches and leaves for cover.

He sat there, his knees huddled under his neck, his arms wrapped about his kneecaps, and tried to blot out the image of Gio's bloodstained body, but it was impossible. He knew the others would be looking for him, to do to him

HECTOR

what they did to Gio, and he wavered between hiding in the bushes until morning or making a run for it and finding a safer spot. In his indecisiveness and panic, he kept locking and unlocking his arms from his knees, readying to stand and run then changing his mind and pulling his body into a tight circle. After a few rounds of that, he forced his body to stand.

His leg felt on fire and he flexed it hard. But it wasn't his muscles hurting; rather the burning sensation was from his pocket, where the cross and chain pressed hard against his thigh. Angrily, Hector reached in and yanked out the necklace. He dangled the chain one last time, watching the metal spin and flash in the air and gritting his teeth as a fiery pain singed his fingertips. Then he hurled it into the bushes and grunted out loud at the image of the Skinny Lady that appeared in his head. She was grinning widely, her skeletal teeth shiny white against a shadow of black. For the first time since Gio's murder, Hector felt at ease.

He pushed his way through branches and brambles until he emerged from the bushes, on the side opposite the lot and for a moment, he stood motionless, surveying the scene. In the distance, a large white cross rising from the top of a cone-shaped structure amid a scattering of small buildings and houses, stood a church.

Go.

It was a single word, a single command, and it splashed across his brain with such force that Hector wasn't sure if it was a thought or a shout. But he felt sure it was the voice of the Skinny Lady, and she was telling him to go to that church.

He stepped surely, with purpose, his eyes fixed unblinkingly straight ahead. He had no fear; he had no thought.

He only knew his Lady was going to protect him and bring him safely to this place of hiding.

Leon slammed his phone down for the fifth time, this time to the ground. He left it there as he paced, then with a loud shout of frustration laced with a string of curse words, he stomped back and bent and retrieved it. He shoved it in his pocket and jumped in his car. With a smooth, fast motion, he revved the engine hard and peeled from the curb, spinning the wheel so he drove in the opposite direction from where he parked.

Within minutes, he saw the truck.

He let his car come to a slow stop in the middle of the road, then sat and stared for several seconds at the driver's seat. He let a few moments pass, then pressed the accelerator and steered for a closer look, taking in the blood, the body, the unnatural rest of Gio's head. An object on the street caught his attention, and after pulling the car toward it, he quickly threw the shifter into park, and jumped out and picked it up, then raced back to his seat and sped from the scene. He pulled down a side street and dialed a number on his phone.

"It's me." Leon's voice was flat and he waited to see if the voice on the end was going to respond. When it didn't, he went on. "It went south. They got Gio." More silence. "Hector's gone." At that, a loud shouting forced Leon to pull the phone a couple inches from his ear. After the voice quieted somewhat, Leon continued talking, his words a rapid stream of nervous chatter.

"I'll find him, Romo. Don't worry. I'll find him." Another minute passed, and Leon pressed the phone close to his ear,

HECTOR

listening hard to Romo's clipped words. He finally nodded and lowered his head in resignation.

"I'll call him. I'll tell him. I'll send him."

He wasn't sure Romo had heard before he was disconnected.

CHAPTER SEVEN

The light from the candles shuddered sporadically in their glass containers, casting waves of pulsating shadows onto the wall. Then, inexplicably, they stopped and sat motionless, waiting for another breath of life to send the flames dancing again. Romo raised a careful hand above the next one in line, and after a few muttered words, struck a match and watched as flame wrought flame and the white one joined the ranks of the black and red ones. He waited until the three candles started smoking, then sat back on his haunches and began muttering once again. From the doorway, Juan watched, his fingers drawn in so tight the nails left little red imprints on his palms. His heart pumped hard and his eyes narrowed in fury as he replayed the news from Leon in his mind. But it was Hector's disappearance, more than Gio's death, that made him seethe. Betrayal demanded a special kind of revenge. Juan knew Romo felt the same and he tapped impatiently with his left foot.

"Here." Romo raised his head and patted the spot on the floor to his left. "She requires sacrifice."

Juan didn't hesitate. He dropped to his knees by the door and crawled toward Romo, head down, a show of proper respect to the Skinny Lady.

Silently, he held his right hand over the golden cup Romo held.

HECTOR

"She requires more." Romo's voice had a strange hollow tone to it and Juan glanced in alarm at his face, then quickly looked away, startled at the two glassy black ovals gazing forth, unblinking, barely human. He put his left hand alongside his right hand, and turned them palms up, wrists exposed. Romo reached onto the altar for a long black blade that rested aside one of the piles of money and with a couple of swift, deft slices, cut into Juan's wrists. He angled the cup in one hand so it captured both flows of blood and with the other, wiped one side of the blade across his cheek then turned it and wiped the other side across Juan's check.

"Drink."

He held the cup to Juan's lips and waited until he swallowed, then raised it to his own mouth and breathed in deeply as he took a drink. He placed the cup at the feet of the Skinny Lady and began to stir the remaining contents slowly, ceremoniously, with the tip of the blade, chanting strange words in a deep monotone. Juan listened with head bowed, his wrists pressed tightly in the shape of an "X" against the center of his chest.

Suddenly, Romo cried out and raised his arms straight into the air, the knife still clutched in his hand. Juan raised his head just in time to see a single drop of blood fall from the blade. It hit the altar and sizzled a fiery red, before turning black then disappearing in a trail of smoke. Romo fell flat to the floor and moaned.

"She has answered. She will find him. She will bring him home," he said, gasping as if the words pained him to utter.

From across the miles, a clank of metal broke the silence of Hector's darkened room, followed by a loud "Caw." Its beady eyes aglow, the crow hopped to the sill of a window that swung open, as if by command, then with a flutter of wings, it disappeared into the night air. It flew higher and higher, making circles in the sky, until something seemed to capture its attention and it swooped. Without slowing, it dove into bushes and for a moment, all was silent. Then with a squawk, the crow sailed back into the sky, a long silver chain trailing from a cross it clutched in its beak flashing and bobbing with each beat of its wings.

At the foot of the altar, Romo raised his face and turned to Juan with a sick smile, made all the more grotesque by the rim of dried blood around his lips from where he drank from the cup.
"She will bring him home," he repeated, his voice even once again. "She will bring him home."
Romo stood, then stared into the Skinny Lady's empty eyes. Finally, he turned to Juan and reached into his pocket and pulled out a set of car keys.
"But just in case," he said, brusquely, "let's go."

Every other possible entryway had been locked tight and Hector was just about to give up on the Skinny Lady, when he saw a lone window peeking through the shrubbery. He stumbled in the bushes alongside the church, putting out a hand and bracing himself against the windowpane just in time to keep from falling. He cursed his stupidity and took a deep breath. Crouching low, he ran his fingers beneath the lip of the window and tugged gently. The window stuck fast then with a groan, as if rudely awakened from a welcome time of slumber, shot up a couple inches. Hector stifled a shout.
"Thank you," he whispered to his Lady, as he scooted low along the ground and measured his shoulders against

HECTOR

the sides of the window. It would be a tight fit. But with a smile, he poked in first his head, then his shoulders, and once his arms were free, he braced them against the inside wall and shimmied in the rest of his body. Carefully, he slipped to the floor and immediately turned to shut the window. It wouldn't do any good, he knew, to have a security guard or police officer happen on the open window and search for intruders. He glanced around the darkened cellar for alarms, then let out a slight chuckle and immediately relaxed. There would be no security concerns about the cellar, he told himself. The space was filled with nothing but junk and cobwebs and dusty, old books. The one piece of furniture, a wooden seaman's chest, was so ancient the slats on the cover curved upwards, revealing its insides to those who would care to peek. Hector glanced down and saw it was stuffed with more books.

"Books and cobwebs," he muttered, running a finger on the wood then feeling with disgust the dust sticking to his skin. His eye fell on several piles of clothing haphazardly lined against the wall, taking up about six feet of space. He drew closer and saw the clothes were sitting on top of an old metal cot covered by a dark green wool blanket, the kind sold in an Army surplus store. He smiled in relief. He wouldn't have to sleep on the cement floor.

Hector sifted through the piles of clothing and pulled out three heavy sweatshirts, then moved the remaining onto the floor, being careful to keep them folded. He fashioned two of the sweatshirts into the shape of a square, one on top of the other, and then wrapped the third around his body. Placing the square at the head of the cot, he drew back the blanket and slipped beneath. He let out a long sigh as he dropped onto his makeshift pillow and pulled the wool blanket until it rested tight beneath his chin. It itched a little,

84

so he took a bit of the sweatshirt and buffered it between his skin and the blanket. He lay there, legs straight, arms drawn against his sides, fingers drawn in little fists in the space between his chin and neck—he lay there, barely breathing, and stared. The images began immediately.

The first was of a bloody windshield beyond which rested the bloodied face of Gio, his head cocked unnaturally sideways, like a dummy in a clothing store whose handlers had yet to readjust its body parts after changing its outfit; and the second, equally disturbing—the smoky gray eyes of a girl whose lifeless body was sprawled across a city street, her fingers molded into a permanent curve as if she had been grasping at something but was suddenly frozen. Hector blinked hard, trying to rid his mind of the pictures. He knew from experience the attempt was fruitless. The eyes never left and now, lying in the damp basement on a creaky cot, Hector fought to chase away the steady streams of Gio's face invading his mind—grotesque images of the before-after—of the moments before the shooting and the terrifying seconds that followed.

Angrily, he smashed the palms of his hands against his forehead, trying to force away the thoughts.

"Ow!" He missed and hit his eye by mistake, and the pain, though not intense, became his vent for all the day's events; for all the horrible events leading up to the day's events, beginning with Gio's tragic shooting and his own flight from the scene and going backward, all the way to the murder of his parents and his abduction by the drug traffickers. In the darkness of the room, Hector's groans, first hushed, coming as almost a rhythmic accompaniment to the massaging of his injured eye, began steadily to morph into moans of despair, then sobs of grief and rage, until finally his pent-up fury took over and he started screaming out

HECTOR

loud, at the top of his voice. He didn't know what words he used, but he peppered them with punches at the cement block wall, his fist striking harder and harder until he heard a crack and, in wonder, looked at the redness and swelling on the back of his hand. He felt nothing, not even a throb, not even after he saw his flesh ripped open and blood flowing off his fingers.

Oh, that's going to hurt, he told himself. But the thought only registered in his mind and went no further.

His face burned hot and he sucked in deeply through his nose, trying to swallow but gagging on his own fluids. Choking, he called on the one thing that had helped him get through the last few hours.

"Lady! My Lady!" He called her over and over, his panic rising when she didn't come. It was as if she were hiding from him, mocking him. Every time he tried to bring her face into focus in his mind, a huge door would slam shut and his mind turned black.

"Lady! Help me, Lady!"

His cries eventually turned to muffled moans until finally, exhausted, he turned on his side, drew his legs tight into his chest, and with his injured hand tucked softly into a pocket, dropped into a fitful sleep.

He was awakened by the insistent shaking of a hand on his shoulder.

"Who are you?"

✳ ✳ ✳

"You still haven't told us who you are."

Hector watched as the woman who woke him wrapped white gauge around his hand and gingerly applied the metal clip to keep it from unraveling. His whole arm throbbed now, and he wondered idly if he had rolled onto his hand while he slept, worsening its injury. But he kept his lips shut tight at the man's questions. He figured the police were on the way and he imagined whatever words he spoke would make their way back to Juan, or worse, Romo. Doing jailtime for breaking and entering might be unpleasant, but facing the wrath of Romo could prove deadly.

"My name is James Clark."

Hector kept his head down, his teeth clenched to keep from groaning out loud. The throbbing was getting worse.

"It's Pastor James Clark, actually. But you can call me Jim. My friends all call me Jim." He smiled, but Hector stayed quiet. "You're in my office right now, at Friendship Christian Church."

Beads of sweat began to congeal on Hector's forehead, banding together to make little rivers that trickled down the side of his face. He shifted slightly, trying to distract himself from the pain.

"This is Mrs. Gable. She found you in the basement—as you know." Pastor James paused. "She heard screaming and when she went to check, she found you tossing and turning and shouting in your sleep." He paused again. "You were screaming, but you were still sleeping."

Hector cleared his throat but said nothing.

"And then when she woke you, she said you just sat there staring at her, with really wide eyes, and said nothing. But she also said something else. You want to know what else she said?" Pastor James watched Hector's face for reaction. Leaning forward a bit in his chair and lowering his voice, he then went on, "She said you looked so frightened she jumped back a couple feet. She said maybe you thought she was a ghost and that's why you looked so frightened. But she said you had the strangest look in your eyes, like a wild

HECTOR

animal who had been beaten and caged for years, and just escaped, and that maybe you thought she was coming to put you back in the cage." Pastor James leaned back again and stared, trying to connect with Hector's lowered eyes.

"Isn't that an interesting thing for her to think," James finally said, shrugging.

Mrs. Gable finished her work on Hector's hand and, with a glance at Pastor James and a short nod, collected her first aid supplies and stood. With a quick pat at Hector's arm, she turned and walked from the room. Pastor James regarded Hector in silence, taking in the bandaged hand, the dirtied clothes, the slight scratches on his cheek.

"Your hand's the size of a melon," he finally said, pointing at the ball of gauze. "We're not sure if it's broken."

When Hector still didn't respond, James sighed and clapped his hands together, as if settling on a decision.

"I'm not going to the police, you know."

At that, Hector raised his head. Pastor James gave a small smile and added, "But I would like to take you to get medical attention for your hand. You could have a broken bone, maybe more. And then maybe you'd like something to eat and then get cleaned—"

"No." It was the first word Hector spoke, and Pastor James opened his eyes wide in surprise. He bit his tongue to keep from saying something sarcastic and instead asked, "No, you don't want something to eat? No, you don't want a shower?"

"No," Hector said, looking squarely into the deep blue of Pastor James's eyes. For a second, Hector thought of the ocean waters of his youth, where he and his father spent so many days walking and fishing. Then he remembered his father on the kitchen floor, prostate and still, and the peaceful waves disappeared and he grit his teeth hard.

"No, I don't need a doctor." His tone was tight and he glared at Pastor James, as if daring him to disagree. But his hand throbbed and he lowered his eyes to hide the tears he could feel welling.

"Look, if you don't want to go to the hospital, at least let me call my friend. He's a doctor, he'll come here if I ask, and he can at least help check and see if your hand is broken. And if it is broken, maybe he could do something to help with that, at least until you're ready to go to the hospital." He waited a moment, watching as Hector gnawed his lip. "You don't want your hand getting deformed, do you? If you don't get that taken care of, it's possible you may never be able to use it again. My friend can come here, fix you up, then be on his way. No police. No medical records. No hassle." Pastor James chuckled. "It's like a doctor's house call, the way it used to be."

Hector swallowed hard, fighting off a loud moan. He felt uncomfortably hot and the room was starting to spin. He looked at his hand and touched the gauze lightly with his finger. Even that slight pressure made him wince. He cleared his throat and swallowed hard. He would need two good hands to fight off Romo and Juan when they found him.

"Okay," he said in a whisper. Bits of sweat fell from his head onto the table, making tiny little popping sounds as they landed.

James regarded him silently for a moment then stood and patted him on the shoulder.

"It'll be all right."

He stepped into the hall and pulled out his phone. After a few minutes, he poked his head back into his office and tapped lightly on the door to get Hector's attention. Hector had slipped low into his chair, his head tilted all the way back, one hand cradling the other.

HECTOR

"Hey, he's on his way."

Hector struggled to sit up and when he failed, let his head drop back against the chair. But he nodded and gave a wave with his good hand.

"I've just got to make one more call, and then I'll bring you something to drink and eat if you want. Then maybe we can talk for a bit, if you're feeling up to it."

Hector shut his eyes again and held back a groan. The last thing he wanted to do was talk. But his hand pounded so hard it felt as if his whole arm was about to explode and he doubted he could stand without fainting or falling. From the darkness of his mind, he heard James's voice from the hallway.

"Hey, Chloe, how are you? How's math camp going? Good? Good. Listen, I've got something to . . ."

James's voice trailed off as the door shut. Weakly, Hector wondered, *Who's Chloe?* Then a final groggy, disjointed thought, before sleep overcame: *I hope her eyes aren't gray.*

CHAPTER EIGHT

"Feeling better?"

James grinned as Hector nodded sleepily, his body spread lazily on the bed, his dark eyes only half opened as they peered at his surroundings. The room was sparsely furnished, containing only a chair with a couple of pillows and a yellow fringed blanket draped over the arm; a small table with lamp and nothing else; a dresser upon which were scattered several books, the titles of which Hector couldn't quite make out; and then another set of drawers matching the wood of the bureau. On top was set an old-fashioned radio with large black knobs, and Hector gazed with interest at the item. He hadn't seen such a radio since his childhood, at the shack of the old man where he and his father used to buy their bait. The thought made him shudder and he gripped his fingers tight, feeling the soft crinkle of the white comforter beneath his body. He looked at his wrapped hand, wondering idly where the throbbing had gone.

As if reading his mind, Pastor James said, "The doctor gave you some pretty good painkillers. You've been asleep for hours."

Hector watched as James walked into the room and beckoned at the chair.

HECTOR

"You mind?" James didn't wait for an answer but plopped onto the cushion, sighing loudly as he stretched his arms along the sides. "So, the good news is your hand isn't broken."

Hector bit his lip and looked to the window above his head. Outside, green leaves fluttered lightly on their branches, and the sun beamed golden from the sky. His head rested on something so soft it felt as if it were disconnected from his body. Or, maybe, he thought with a wry uptick of his lips, it was the drugs the doctor gave him. Either way, he hadn't felt so calm in—he couldn't remember when. The realization brought a lump to his throat. Embarrassed and confused, Hector kept his eyes fixed steadily on the leaves, but he listened intently, nevertheless, to what James was saying.

"The bad news, though, is your hand is going to hurt you for quite a while. It'll probably be a couple weeks before the swelling goes down enough that you can take off the wrap, except to ice it. And in the meanwhile, you're going to have to keep it as immobile as you can, and keep it elevated as frequently as you can." James tapped lightly on the two pillows next to him, shoved deeply down the side of the chair. "You'll probably want these at night to lay your arm on so your wrist and hand stay elevated. You might even want to tie a light rope or ribbon or something around your arm onto the pillows, so it helps keep your hand from falling off and smacking onto the bed—which doesn't sound bad but I'm betting you're swollen enough it would hurt like the devil." James smiled. "See what I did there?"

Hector turned and stared, his face expressionless. James, unperturbed, smiled broader. He leaned forward and scooted his chair closer to the bed. The scratching of wood on wood grated loudly and Hector opened his mouth to speak then, just as quickly, clamped his lips tight. His mother's voice called in his mind.

"Hector, pick up the chair! Don't slide it across the floor!"

He turned back to the window, the dark shadow crossing his face not going unnoticed by James. When James next spoke, his voice was very soft.

"Who's the Skinny Lady?"

Hector shifted so quickly toward James he hit his hand on his side and shouted the first words that came to mind. Panicked, he started to apologize. James raised his hand and shook his head.

"It's fine. No need to apologize." His voice was the same soft level, and Hector lay his head back on the pillow and watched while James moved his chair even closer.

"Look," he said, after a long pause, his eyes fixed directly on Hector's. He took Hector's attention as a positive sign and he cleared his throat, choosing his words carefully and speaking as if he were trying to soothe a frightened child. "Mrs. Gable heard you. She said when she went into the basement, she saw you thrashing and kicking on the cot as if you were fighting off something, or someone." He paused to let that sink in, and when he saw Hector was still listening, he gave a few sympathetic nods before continuing.

"She also said you were screaming out the words, 'Skinny Lady, save me, Lady, save me, Lady, Skinny Lady, save me,' over and over and over."

Hector's eyes widened but he still said nothing.

"Now I don't know for sure—maybe Skinny Lady is a nickname of one your friends, or maybe a relative or someone else who's close to you." Pastor James reached out to lay his hand on the bed, just inches from Hector's

HECTOR

arm. "But the only Skinny Lady I know is the one who is also called the saint of death, the one who is worshipped by members of a cult who think a skeleton figure dressed in bright cloth will save them from having to face the consequences of their evil deeds." James's words were blunt but his tone was softer than ever.

"And do you know who usually worships this skeleton as a god?" he asked quietly. His eyes were brilliant blue and he fixed them on Hector's brown ones as he answered his own question. "Drug dealers. Traffickers. Criminals." He reached forward and touched Hector very lightly. "Or," he said, letting his hand rest on Hector's arm, "people who don't know better."

Hector blinked, then kept his eyes shut for so long, James wondered if he were dozing off. He moved his hand to give a gentle shake to his shoulder but before he could, Hector peeled open his lids. James sucked in his breath. Hector's eyes were brimming with water. Astonished, James watched first one tear then another slide down his face until Hector, wracked with grief, burst forth sobs so powerful the bed shook.

"It's okay, it's okay, it's okay." James wrapped his arms as best he could around Hector's shoulder and chest, pulling tighter with each passing second. He felt Hector's body shift and then an arm squeeze about his neck, and for several minutes they sat that way, and James rocked very lightly in tune with his words.

"It's okay, it's okay, it's okay."

Hector's weeping finally began to slow, the convulsing left his body, and his cries dimmed until they turned to gasps. After several minutes, the room quieted and the only sounds James heard was a slight whistle from the rising and falling of Hector's chest, along with intermittent sniffling.

Carefully, James slipped his head back a couple inches and as he did, the grip on his arm loosened. Hector breathed in deep through his nose, sniffing hard then swallowing noisily. James took that as his cue and sat up straight. But he kept his one hand on Hector's arm, rubbing soothingly with his fingertips.

"Do you want to tell me your name now?"

Hector looked at James and nodded.

"Hector." He sniffled and wiped his face with his hand. "My name is Hector Menendez."

"Well, good to meet you, Hector Menendez. My name, as I previously mentioned, is James Clark. Actually, Pastor James Clark. But you can call me Jim. My friends all call me Jim."

Hector nodded again but didn't say anything.

"Hey, you hungry now? You want something to eat?"

James didn't wait for an answer. He stood, scratching the chair legs across the floor and leaving a trail of tiny lines in the wood.

"Of course you're hungry. I'll get you something. The kitchen's right down the hall. I'll be right back."

Hector cleared his throat.

"Thank you," he finally said just as James was opening the door to leave. He didn't see James's triumphant smile, only that he paused to show he heard.

"Be right there." The door clicked lightly behind him and Hector sighed heavily, looking to his wrapped hand with relief; the painkillers were still doing their job. A shadow outside his window caught his attention and he glanced just in time to see two jet black wings take flight. Hector's lips formed into a perfect circle as he caught his breath and lifted his head in surprise. He couldn't tell for certain, but the bird that had just flown off the tree limb and past the

HECTOR

frame of the window, out of his line of sight, looked just like a crow. He cocked his head to the side and strained to sit. But the bird was gone. Exhausted, Hector flopped back on his bed and burrowed his head from side to side in his pillow, listening to the slight crunch his hair made on the cool cotton sheet. Inexplicably, he shivered and with his good hand, he pat tight the comforter around his neck. Two angry red eyes bored into his mind and he shuddered again. The Skinny Lady was coming for him. He knew she wouldn't be long.

"Here you go." The door banged open and James's cheery voice echoed in the room. Hector opened his eyes in surprise. He hadn't realized he drifted into sleep. He watched as James placed a tray on the bureau, then walked to the closet and removed a folding chair. He placed the chair alongside the bed, right by Hector's chest, then carefully laid the tray on the chair. Then he pulled up his own chair, scratching lines in the wood floor once again. When he was directly opposite Hector, he lifted a plate and held it in both hands.

"Sandwiches, chips, cookies." He helped Hector balance the plate on his lap. "It's not fancy, but it is good."

James watched as Hector picked up the sandwich and bit, first hesitantly, chewing slowly, and then ravenously, as if he hadn't eaten in weeks. In the span of just a few seconds, the sandwich was gone and Hector was shoving chips in his mouth, so many at a time that they puffed his cheeks and little crumbs spurt from his lips as he munched. Smiling, Pastor James picked up his own sandwich and placed it on Hector's plate.

CHERYL CHUMLEY

"You know, I'm not really hungry. I only made myself a sandwich to keep you company while you ate, but honestly, I ate earlier." He gestured as Hector paused, staring at his plate. "Go ahead. I've got this." He cracked open a soda and sucked deeply at the can.

"Thanks," Hector mumbled, already tearing into the bread.

James wiped his mouth then licked the side of the can where soda had spilled and dripped. He patted his stomach as if he were full and with a tiny smooth movement, made with the point of his index finger, pushed his plate with cookies and chips toward Hector.

"Go ahead. I don't want them to go to waste."

Hector finished his own cookies then reached for James's plate. He ate more slowly now, his head rested peacefully against the pillow, barely lifting it as he brought the food to his mouth, pausing in between bites to take sips of his own soda. Finally, he finished and with a sigh of satisfaction, placed the empty can back on the chair alongside the two plates. He turned to James and for the first time, his forehead was smooth of wrinkles and his mouth, while not quite turned into a smile, was no longer grimacing. Pastor James noted the difference and sat back in his chair, relaxing into a position of crossed legs.

"How are you feeling, Hector?"

Hector nodded, then raised his wrapped hand and cradled it with his other.

"Thank you for this," he said, a smile brightening his face as he nodded more. "I don't know what came over me. I don't really know what happened. But I know my hand was killing me and now it isn't and I just want to say thank you."

He raised his head and grinned shyly at James, then ducked down again.

HECTOR

"Thank you."

His words were barely above a whisper but James caught their sincerity and on impulse, he reached forward and ruffled Hector's hair. Hector looked up in surprise.

"Nobody's done that since my mother died," he blurted.

James peered at Hector's face, trying to make sense of the startling polite demeanor coming from a boy with such dirtied clothes who, a few short hours earlier, had been found screaming and writhing in the basement. Hector's eyes, now soft, nonetheless contained a wild shadowy layer that spoke of dark secrets, and they were rimmed with tiny wrinkles that couldn't have come from age; James guessed he was only about fifteen or sixteen years old.

"Tell me about her." James kept his voice quiet but he purposely made it a statement, not a question.

After a long moment of silence, Hector began speaking.

"Her name was Earlina. And she was the best mother you could have," he said sadly. "She used to make me and my dad breakfast every morning and then we'd sit at the table and start the day talking about all the stuff we had to do. My dad would drink coffee and she would drink tea. And every time, she always asked if I had my homework done—always, every morning. Even when she knew I had it finished, she always asked." Hector gave a short laugh. "It used to bug the sh—" He glanced at James and grimaced. "Sorry. I mean, it used to bug the heck out of me she'd always ask, every day, every day, every day, 'Hector, you finish your school work?' 'Yes, yes, Mama, I finished my school work.' Then she'd say, 'Hector, you have your school work in your bag?' 'Yes, yes, Mama, my school work is in my bag.' Then she'd go, 'Hector, you have your bag by the door so you don't forget it?' 'Yes, yes, Mama, yes, my bag is by the door; I won't forget it.'"

Hector smiled, lost in his memory.

"Then she'd notice I was getting annoyed and she'd keep up the questions, just to annoy me more." Hector pressed his lips tight and cocked his head at James. "That's what she did, you see. She liked to annoy me like that because she thought it was funny. 'Hector, you have a pencil in your bag with your homework?' 'Yes, yes, Mama, I got my pencil.' 'Hector, you have your homework in a nice folder so it doesn't get dirty in your bag?' 'Yes, Mama, my homework papers are in a nice folder.' It'd go on like that for a while longer and then, then when she knew I was good and aggravated, then she'd ask me something like, 'Hector, how come your teacher called me yesterday and told me you didn't turn in your homework?' And I'd pretend to be shocked and I'd say, 'That's not true, Mama. I turned in all my homework yesterday.' And then she'd say, 'Hector, are you calling your teacher a liar? That is very disrespectful, Hector. Why would your teacher lie to me?'"

Hector laughed out loud, growing more animated as he recounted to James how his father would sometimes chime in and ask if she wanted him to go to the school and confront the teacher for lying; or how his father other times might then turn on Hector and feign indignation for falsely accusing the teacher of lying.

"Every day," Hector said, wiping his hand over his mouth, "every day it was something different." He sniffed. "But then again, every day was the same too."

He sighed heavily.

"The last time was the day before she was murdered."

James gasped.

"Oh!" His hand shot to his mouth and he kept it there, fingers over lips, for several seconds, watching Hector with huge widened eyes.

HECTOR

Hector stared at the wall off the foot of his bed for a long time. When he spoke again, his words were clipped and angry, and his hand clenched into a tight ball against his side.

"Me and my dad came home and found her body in the kitchen. The cartel was still in the house. And as soon as they saw us, they grabbed my dad and killed him too." Hector choked as he continued. "There was blood everywhere. There was blood on the floor, on the cabinets. On their faces." He struggled to breath. "Then they grabbed me and shoved me in their car. They told me I had a new home now." Hector turned to James with dead eyes. "And I been here ever since working for them."

"Working for them?" James shook his head back and forth. "Oh my God. Doing what?"

"What you think?" Hector spit out the question and his voice rose so suddenly, James leaned back in his chair. "I got no choice!" Hector smacked hard on the mattress with his fist and his face contorted in fury. "They made me! They made me! You don't know, man—you just don't know!"

James waited a few seconds, but Hector clamped his lips tight and turned toward the wall, his angry words still thundering across the room.

"Hey." James spoke quietly, but something about his tone caught Hector's attention and he turned his head—and when he did, he saw a face filled with such compassion and kindness the fight went out of him and his body deflated. He sank his head deep into his pillow and breathed out deeply, unclenching his hands and letting his fingers glide smoothly along the coolness of the comforter.

"Tell me." James leaned forward, elbows on knees, and folded his hands beneath his chin. "Tell me everything that happened. It's okay." He lay a gentle hand on Hector's arm.

CHERYL CHUMLEY

"'For we do not have a high priest who is unable to sympathize with our weaknesses, but one who in every respect has been tempted as we are, yet without sin. Let us then with confidence draw near to the throne of grace, that we may receive mercy and find grace to help in time of need.'" James finished speaking and nodded slightly at Hector, taking in his wide eyes and attentive expression. "That's from Hebrews, chapter 4, verses 15 and 16. Have you heard it before? It means Jesus has faced every sort of trial and tribulation and temptation we have and He understands firsthand whatever it is you're going through; whatever it is you're facing. You can trust Him completely. You can trust that He is dependable and reliable and always there for you and if you only confess your sins and tell Him your heart and mind, He will be faithful and respond, in love, and will help you. Do you know what grace is?"

James didn't wait for Hector's reply.

"It's underserved favor. It's getting God's favor and blessing and help even though you don't deserve it. Even though you know you don't deserve it. Even when you think you've done something so bad, there's no possible way you deserve it. And guess what, Hector?"

Hector bit his lip and raised his brows, as if awaiting the answer.

"None of us deserve it. So there's really nothing you could say or do that would take away your ability to accept God's grace. The only thing is—you have to want it. You have to realize it's a gift, a free gift from God, and you have to accept that gift. And honestly, that's the hardest part. That's the part where the devil tries to deceive and tell you what you've done is so bad God won't forgive you and what you've done is so terrible you can't get God's grace and blessings. It's the devil who whispers to you you're worse

HECTOR

than everyone else and somehow, you're the exception—the one who's done something so wrong you don't get the same treatment from God as the rest of the people in the world."

Hector took a deep breath, then let it out loudly. When he was finished, he picked up his soda can, sucking at the remaining drops. Then he put it carefully on the chair and gazed at James for a few moments, searching his eyes for the key that would unlock his fate.

"Don't listen to that voice any longer, Hector. That Skinny Lady? She doesn't love you and she's not looking out for you. She can't grant you grace. She can't give you forgiveness. She can't give you anything but more of the grief and turmoil and trouble that's been plaguing you—that's so obviously thrown your whole life into this dark path."

"She brought me here, didn't she?" Hector shot the words out of his mouth without thinking. He stared at Pastor James with narrowed eyes. "She was the one who told me to come here. She was the one who showed me the window to go into the cellar and she was the one who got me away from—"

Hector shut his mouth tight and clamped his teeth.

"Away from who? Away from what?" James regarded Hector solemnly. "And did she really, Hector? Did your Skinny Lady really bring you here, to this church, to this place of worship of Christ—or was it more you saw this church and thought it a good place to hide and then in your mind, you imagined it was your Skinny Lady who showed you this church, so you gave thanks to her?"

Hector scrunched his mouth, tracing the events of that night.

"Perhaps," James went on, crossing his arms over his chest, "perhaps it wasn't your Skinny Lady who led you here at all." He looked closely to gauge Hector's reaction.

"Perhaps," he said, his words at first coming slowly, then speeding as he finished his thought, "perhaps it was actually God who led you here, not your Skinny Lady. And perhaps God led you here because He knew you would meet a pastor who would tell you the truth about false gods and help lead you down the right path to Christ."

Hector started to say something, then the words of his father came to him and he instead caught his breath in his throat and looked at Pastor James with wet eyes.

"My dad used to talk about how God would never leave or forsake him." Hector looked down and pursed his lips into a tight line. "Then he was murdered." When he raised his head again, his eyes were wet and rimmed in red. "Sounds to me like God left him. And my mother too."

"I can see how you would think that, Hector." James nodded in sympathy. "Probably anyone in your shoes would think that too. It was a horrible thing that happened to your parents. It's a horrible thing that brought you here, I'm sure—and I'd like to hear all about everything. I'd like to know what it was you were running from that brought you to my church. But Hector, you have to realize." He sighed and patted Hector on the shoulder. "You have to realize it's not God who took away your parents. Those were the actions of evil men who were listening to evil thoughts and desires—who were listening to the evil one—the same evil one who's trying to get you now to blame God for what's happened to your parents and for what's happened to you. The same evil one who goes by many names, including the name Skinny Lady."

"But God could've stopped it! God could've stopped my parents from being murdered if He wanted to!" Hector smacked his hand hard on the bed as he shouted, not caring if his words offended the pastor or not, and he sucked in

HECTOR

breaths hard and fast as he waited to hear the explanation. But what James said surprised him.

"Hector." James kept his eyes lowered on his lap as he spoke, and his voice was so soft, and laced with sadness, Hector had to strain to hear. "That is the one question everyone in the world, from nonbelievers to pastors of churches, want answered: Why do bad things happen to good people?" James shook his head slowly and raised his eyes, looking into the distance. "And if you ever get the answer to that, I sure wish you'd tell me," James said, with a barely perceptible nod.

The two fell into silence as the wind outside blew, sending the leaves on the tree into jerky motions that scattered strange shadows on the walls. Hector watched the shadows with an odd expression on his face, a mixture of curiosity and anger, as if those dancing figures held the clues that would lead to the solution of an enormous puzzle, but they were purposely keeping them hidden, for their own amusement or for other reasons of even greater secretive nature. He narrowed his eyes until they were tiny slits and the shadows became blurred so he could not tell one from another. Through squinted lids, he tried separating and tracing them in his mind, until the effort bored him and he forgot why he was bothering. He sat up and shot his eyes open wide. The first thing they fell on was a wooden board, about four inches in height and stretching a foot in length, placed at the edge of the bureau. The board was painted a bright garish yellow, and its border was dotted with equally bright and garish red blotches with dots of green. Upon closer inspection, Hector saw the blotches were actually supposed to be flowers. It was very ugly, no doubt the creation of a child, and it stood out among the more traditional, muted design of the room. But on it blared letters, in bold purple capitals: "GOD LOVES YOU."

I wonder why I didn't notice that before, Hector thought idly, feeling a sudden warm tickle course through his body. In shock, he waited for it to pass, and then with a loud exhale, as if arriving at an important decision, he turned his head to James and smiled.

"Okay, then," he said. "You wanna know everything?"

James nodded.

"I sell drugs for the cartel."

They spoke deep into the night, long after the shadows of leaves had stopped dancing and faded into black and the air outside the window darkened enough to hide the trees.

CHAPTER NINE

"I'm telling you, Chloe. He really has had the most horrible experience."

James set the phone on the top of his desk and hit the speaker button, then stretched back in his chair and yawned loudly.

"Oh, thanks for that," Chloe said sarcastically, a note of laughter floating through the receiver.

James chuckled too, and reached for his coffee cup.

"Sorry. That was rude. But in my defense, I haven't gotten much sleep these past few weeks. Between regular church business and talking with Hector and helping him to his doctor appointments, and getting him settled, it's been a very busy time." He took a gulp then choked. The coffee was too hot and he jumped, spilling some on his lap.

"It will be good when you get back," he said, wiping at his pants with a rolled-up piece of paper he grabbed from the pile.

"Should be later this evening. Camp is finishing this morning, but I have a couple stops to make on the drive." Loud coughing filled the line, and James pulled back the phone from his ear.

"Sorry," she said. "But I guess we're even now." Chloe cleared her throat. "So I have about an hour before I have

HECTOR

to meet the group. Tell me the latest on Hector. He's been staying in my old room?"

"The very one. Yes."

"It's turning into a sort of refuge, isn't it?"

For answer, James sighed.

"Has it really been two years?" he asked, speaking just as much to himself as to Chloe.

Chloe smiled, forgetting he couldn't see her. She ticked off the months in her head.

"Almost two years, yes. Time flies—when you're paying off DUI tickets and healing from a broken leg," she added, with a small chuckle.

"You've come a long way, Chloe. I couldn't be prouder."

"Well," she said quietly, "it isn't many people who'd give me the second chance you did. Hector's in good hands. I hope he knows . . ."

Her words trailed off as she thought back to her old room—the one Hector was currently occupying—and recalled her first days at the church, and her first time meeting James. He was actually the other driver in an alcohol-related car crash she caused, a crash leading to her trouble with the police, her broken leg and hospitalization, her loss of job and income, and her eventual loss of home. Thankfully, James hadn't been injured, and instead visited at the hospital and invited her to stay and recover at the church. Once he discovered her talent for math, he'd even given her a job as an accountant for the church finances, and later, as a math teacher for the Christian school he also headed.

Along the way, he also taught her about God.

Even now, she couldn't think back on the mess her life had been when she was an atheist, and the upward trajectory it took since meeting James and since becoming a Christian, without a ball forming in her throat.

108

"I hope this guy knows how lucky he is right now," Chloe said more forcefully, tightening her fingers around the phone.

"We call it blessings, not luck, remember, Chloe?" James laughed as he spoke. But Chloe knew he meant what he said.

"Yes. It's all from God. All glory to God," she said somberly.

"All glory to God," James repeated, then abruptly changed the subject. "So let me tell you a little bit more about Hector. How much time did you say you had? I want to tell you how he finally agreed to talk to the police. Oh— and guess what. He says he's never been baptized. He was raised in a Christian home but since he lost his parents, he's been angry with God and started to turn toward a cultish figure, a skeletal figure—a demonic figure, really—called the Skinny Lady. But his heart's not on pagan worship. I think he really wants to return to God; he just struggles with understanding why his parents were taken from him and why God let all this happen in his life. You know," James said, a wry tone in a voice, "the easy stuff to answer."

The line went silent a moment, and then they both spoke at the same time.

"I think maybe you might be able to help—"

"I think I might be able to help him—" Chloe laughed, then finished their thought. "Yeah, I think maybe when I get back I could sit down and talk with him about bad things happening to good people and how you can get past that."

James smiled.

"I knew you'd want to share your story to help him," he said, getting up from his chair and walking toward the kitchen for another cup of coffee.

Hector quickly ducked into the office next to James's and slipped behind the door. He watched through the crack

HECTOR

as James entered the kitchen, then quickly he stepped into the hallway and raced back to his own room. He heard everything or at least everything James said, which was enough to piece together how Chloe responded on her own end. He wondered what this woman could possibly tell him that would make him change his mind about God. It's not that he wanted to see God as unconcerned and removed, unwilling to save innocent people from evil acts. His father and mother, after all, taught him God was loving and all-knowing, and that with prayer, all things were possible. But he couldn't move past the images of his bloodied parents on the kitchen floor and see how it was possible God could be both loving and all-knowing, yet allow such travesty to occur. His mother prayed every day, for crying out loud! And his father—his father spent years as a law enforcement officer fighting evil, fighting the drug traffickers, fighting the cartels, and what did it get him? The day he visited a poor woman and gave her money was the very day he was brutally murdered by the cartel. The same day he was doing God's work, was the same day God abandoned him and let the evil destroy all. Whose side was God on, anyway?

The question made Hector seethe, and he clenched his fists hard and tried to keep the hot tears from falling.

He stretched out his legs and lay flat on his back on his bed, breathing deeply and letting go his rage, counting to ten as Pastor James counseled. He shut his eyes and tried to remember the story of Job and the details of how he trusted God and refused to condemn Him, even though he lost his children, his wealth, his health, his reputation. He tried to put himself in Job's shoes and how it feels to lose everything for no apparent reason and to still trust in God.

"Though He slay me, I will hope in Him," Hector whispered, recalling the memory verse James had given him from the book of Job. He repeated it over and over, again and again, until his body relaxed and his fingers unfurled and his breathing returned to normal.

"Though He slay me, I will hope in Him, though He slay me, I will hope in Him, though He slay me, I will hope in Him," he said. "Chapter 13, verse 15, though He slay me, I will hope in Him, though He slay me, I will hope in Him, chapter 13 verse 15, though He slay me . . ."

His mind drifted to the last day of his father's life and to their drive back from the poor woman's home and to the answer he received to a question that had long puzzled him. He asked his father how he managed to keep from shooting and killing the cartel members he arrested and brought to jail, and made the comment that ridding the world of such scum would be a favor to the world, and then his father looked at him with such a serious expression, he shut his mouth tight.

"Hector, I am an officer of the law, not an executioner," his father said. "But more than that, I am not their judge. Only God can judge."

And Hector blurted, "Well even God must hate drug dealers."

"Hector," his father said again, very quietly. "What you are really asking is how can I treat a drug dealer the same as I treat that poor woman and her children; how can I treat a criminal the same as an innocent. Yes?" He waited for Hector to nod. "Well, every day, when I say my morning prayers, I first thank God for all the blessings of my life— for Earlina, for you, for our home, for the sunshine, for the fish we catch that afternoon, for the food on our plate that evening. Then I pray for the less fortunate. I pray for the forgotten. I pray for God to show me how to be a blessing to the less fortunate and the forgotten. And God shows me

HECTOR

how the criminals I arrest were once tiny babies, fragile and innocent and weak and dependent. And when He shows me that, I realize something went wrong in their lives to bring them to the point of their criminal behavior—and the very something that went wrong in their lives was something I was spared from having to face. And then I thank God because I know, when I look at these drug dealers, when I look at these criminals, when I see such evil on the streets and in the faces of those people I arrest—I know that truly, there but for the grace of God go I."

His father finished this way: "It doesn't make me hate their evil any less. It doesn't make me excuse their evil or think they are innocent of their crimes. But it does make me more compassionate in my heart, and it does make me more grateful for what I have, and it does make me realize—as much as God loves me—well, that's as much as He loves the ones I arrest. And that helps me stay grounded and humble and useful for God."

Hector thought hard on his father's words. Just as they were about to pull down the street toward their home, his father had said one more thing.

"Those criminals are the lost souls and it's not necessarily your job in this life to save them. But it is your job to make sure your own soul never gets lost like that," he said.

"Remember that," his father said. "Always remember that."

Then they pulled into their driveway and Hector had forgotten.

"Hector?"

The tiny knock at his door grew louder. Hector, with a start, opened his eyes. He hadn't realized he was dropping off to sleep.

"Yes? Come in."

The door opened and Pastor James stuck his head inside. His mouth was pulled into a wide smile and his white teeth glistened as he spoke.

"I want to introduce you to Chloe. Finally." He stepped into the room and half-turned, gesturing with his arm toward the woman who followed. She was wearing a green coat with a matching hat, and something about her dark hair and the way she shook her head free of its covering made Hector sit up straight. He looked at her pale white face and sucked in his breath so hard he gasped out loud. She stopped, mid-stride, and stared.

"You!"

Pastor James turned to her in shock as she uttered a string of words better used in a bar.

Hector twisted his body and flung his feet hard to the floor, half-rising then sitting then half-rising once again. He finally settled on the side of the bed, gripping tightly at the comforter and grinding his teeth hard. His eyes met Chloe's and for what seemed an eternity, they watched each other in icy silence. Chloe spoke first, still glaring at Hector.

"This is the a__hole who carjacked us, Jim."

Hector felt more than saw James's head swivel his way.

"This is the guy who stuck a gun in our backs and stole your truck."

CHAPTER TEN

The next few minutes were a blur as Hector jumped from the bed and grabbed his coat off the chair and rushed the door. He sidestepped James, and tried to push past Chloe but she grabbed his sleeve and for several moments, a tug of war ensued. Then his shirt ripped and Hector spun free. In a flash, he was down the hall, the sound of pursuing footsteps thundering in his ear. He didn't dare look back but slammed through the door to the outside world. He kept running across the parking lot, across the grassy field, back the way he had come weeks ago.

He kept running until he felt he was going to vomit, then he crashed to the ground in a gasping heap. Chloe's face flooded his mind, her furious eyes cutting deep and slicing at his heart. His chest thumped and for a few moments, he panicked, wondering if he was going to have a heart attack or some sort of massive stroke that would leave him dead right there, right in the middle of the dirt and bushes and gravel of the abandoned lot. The thought made his chest hurt more. Then he realized the reason he was thinking that, and sadness washed over him.

Hector had spent the last few weeks in such peace he had forgotten what it felt like to live in a constant state of fear.

For the first time since his parents were killed, he lived in a secure and safe environment. He slept deeply, ate

HECTOR

regularly, and spoke softly—because he had been spoken softly to—and he had even prayed daily. The God of his youth, the God his father and mother taught him to love had come back and pushed away the demons of the Skinny Lady. His vision had started to clear and he had begun to see light more than dark, and he had actually started to discuss a future and to plot a future and to believe he could *have* a future.

As Pastor James repeatedly said, through Jesus all things were possible. As Hector healed, he had been finding his faith.

He sat up slowly, brushed the dirt and pebbles from his scratched hands, and took deep breaths to quiet his heart.

That's why, he thought—with a level of sorrow he hadn't felt since looking out the rear car window as the cartel whisked him from the only home he had ever known—*I forgot what it was like to be happy.*

A heavy weight bore down hard on his shoulders and he pulled his knees tight into his chest and gently rocked.

He had no idea what he was going to do now.

❄ ❄ ❄

"You don't recognize him?"

James looked at Chloe's expression of disbelief, her lips pulled open so the tips of her teeth were exposed, and shrugged.

"No. I told you that night I didn't get a good look at the guy. It all happened so fast and plus, I was looking at you to make sure you were okay."

Chloe sighed in frustration.

"That's him! That's the guy! That's the little freaking son of—" She stopped short at the sight of Pastor James's face. "Sorry," she muttered, lowering her head but her tone still angry.

"That's the guy, though. I remember that night like it was yesterday and I remember his face as well as if I were to shut my eyes and remember yours."

James walked to the door and held it for Chloe.

"Let's get a coffee. I'll make a pot. Come on."

Chloe choked back an angry reply and stomped to the door. She paused in front of James to shoot him a look of disgust, then headed down the hallway, not bothering to wait for him. She yanked her chair in the kitchen so hard it knocked over another one. James entered just in time to hear her string of curses. This time, she didn't bother to apologize but rather plopped in the chair and folded her arms across her chest, glaring at a spot on the floor.

"Boy, you can cut the tension with a knife," he joked. When Chloe said nothing, he shrugged and decided some background noise was in order. He walked to the television set in the corner, dug out its remote from the drawer, and flipped the "on" button. Loud voices boomed and hastily, James pushed the volume control. He flicked around the stations a few times, glancing back at Chloe.

"Anything you want to watch?"

She shrugged, her face grim, eyes glued to the floor.

James sighed. "Okay, news it is," he said, turning and placing the remote on the table in front of Chloe, then walking to the coffee pot. He kept his back to her as he worked, watching the flow of liquid as it funneled into the carafe. When it was done brewing and the dripping stopped, he grabbed two white ceramic mugs from the cabinet and poured coffee into them, being careful not to spill any as he carried them to the table. He lay one gently in front of

HECTOR

Chloe then, still standing, took several sips from his. He waited for her to reach for her mug and when she did, watched as she carefully placed her lips on the brim and drank. Swallowing, she looked up at him.

"Are you going to stand there and watch me drink my coffee?" Her tone was sullen, but James just smiled and shook his head.

Sliding into the chair opposite her, he placed his cup on the table and sniffed several times, as if amused by a private thought. Chloe glanced at him, annoyed.

"Something funny?"

"I was just remembering a conversation we had in here a long time ago, when you first came to work here and we were sitting across from each other, getting to know each other a bit." He gulped his coffee, then coughed. "Too hot," he said, wiping his mouth.

Chloe cleared her throat and waited for him to continue, her expression blank.

"Okay, so maybe you remember that day, maybe you don't." He gave her a few seconds to respond, and when she didn't, he hurried to explain. "That was the day I told you about my past—about my dad and how he used to hit my mom, and about how he finally left us and then, we had a hard time because money was always tight. And then how she ended up getting killed by a drunk driver." He paused, his eyes growing distant. Then he shook his head and looked at Chloe, watching as her features softened and her mouth relaxed.

"You do remember."

"Yes," she said quietly. They sat there sipping coffee and staring at their mugs for several moments in silence. Then Chloe reached out a hand and placed it on James's forearm, tapping with her fingers as she spoke.

"But that doesn't mean the guy who held us up at gunpoint and took off with the truck we were driving ought to get a free pass." The tightness was back in her voice and she sat back hard against her chair, bumping the table in the process. Brown liquid shot out of her mug and exasperated, she rubbed at the pool of coffee spreading across the table with her hand, trying to keep it from dripping off the side onto the floor. James stood and grabbed a napkin from the counter and he was about to throw it toward her when something on the television caught his eye. He grabbed the remote off the table and turned up the volume, forgetting all about the napkin in his hand.

"Hey." Chloe grabbed at his hand. "It's making a big mess," she said, pulling the napkin and wiping first her hand, then the table.

"Shh." James stared at the TV, not noticing Chloe's look of surprise. "Wait a minute," he mumbled, pressing the volume button on the remote once again.

". . . and the police say they have found the suspects in the murder of Giovanni Herrara, the man discovered shot and killed in a stolen truck earlier this month. We go now to Captain Simon Bulloch, who's taking to the podium to give us the latest from the police department on this mysterious case."

The television screen flashed away from the news anchor and onto a man in a dark blue police uniform with a badge bearing his name, Bulloch, standing in the middle of three other men and one woman, all similarly dressed. Bulloch unfolded a sheet of paper, laid it on the podium, and then changed his mind and picked it up and began reading. James turned to Chloe and pointed at the television.

"This is what Hector told me about. This is what happened to him."

HECTOR

Chloe nodded, her face growing somber as she listened to Bulloch speak.

"Shh," she said, not noticing James's wry grin.

"On the fifteenth of last month, police responded to an anonymous caller who detailed the discovery of a dead body in a red pickup truck in the vicinity of the Jersey Jett housing community, on Platt Street. Police located the truck, later identified as being stolen, and found inside the body of a male, approximately eighteen-to-twenty-two-years old, with several wounds to his head and torso. Paramedics responding to the scene pronounced the man dead and a coroner later determined his death was due to injuries sustained from gunfire. The man was later identified as Giovanni Herrara, a known gang member and drug dealer. Detectives investigating his death learned the names of several of Herrara's associates and, working in conjunction with a confidential informant, were able to identify the suspects in his murder."

"Hector was the informant," James said, turning his head quickly to Chloe, who nodded.

"Following weeks of undercover work by the special drugs suppression task force detectives, I am proud to say police have arrested the two suspects in Herrara's murder. They are Juan Diagarza, age twenty-eight, and Romo Salavado, age thirty-three, both of no particular fixed address but with past ties to several towns south of the border known for heavy cartel activity. As the investigation continues and there are more suspects police are seeking, I am not able to take questions at this time. But I would like to point to the stellar work of the detectives and task force team who were . . ."

James reduced the volume and turned to Chloe, his mouth moving in rapid time as he rushed to fill in the details.

120

CHERYL CHUMLEY

"This is what I told you Hector was talking to the police about. This is what Hector agreed—finally—to meet with the police about. He told his whole story, about how his parents were murdered and he was taken by cartel members and carted across the border and set up with Gio and another guy—I guess they don't have that guy arrested yet; his name is Leon, I think—but how he was put in a house that was in a really run-down condition, like maybe it had been abandoned or something. And he wasn't allowed to leave the house because he was kept there against his will by a guy named Juan." James gestured excitedly at the television screen, which now showed the news anchor behind her desk once again, and in the upper right corner the booking photos of the arrested suspects who had apparently been provided by police. "That's that guy—that's Juan. The police arrested him, and the other guy, Romo, well Hector said Romo was Juan's boss. So they got him too."

Chloe sipped slowly at her coffee mug and gazed at the faces of the two men staring back at her from the screen, their expressions dark, their eyes black as midnight. She shuddered, imagining a life where she was trapped in a house with the man named Juan as her guard.

"The windows were painted black," James was saying, as Chloe stared at Juan's menacing glare.

How old is Hector, anyway? she thought, biting her bottom lip nervously.

An image of her angry father, drunk on whiskey, leapt to Chloe's mind and she froze, coffee mug to mouth, her lips half open as if about to sip. She clamped her mouth tight as the memory unfolded.

The snow had been swirling and Chloe, excited at the prospect of a white Christmas, had been dawdling behind

HECTOR

her dad, twisting her tongue into contortions as she tried to catch flakes as they walked.

"Hurry up." Her father's rough voice cut through the wind. He was more tense than usual and Chloe rushed, forgetting all about the snowflakes as she hurried to his side. A strong gust lifted her hat and carried it into a crowd of Christmas tree shoppers. Chloe paused, watching it bump across the snow, but then decided to let it go. Her father's long strides were hard enough to keep pace with as it was, and she didn't dare stop and fall farther behind him. She huffed with the effort of plowing through a foot of wet snow, lifting first one heavy boot, then another, and the small beads of sweat trickling down her forehead were stinging her eyes.

"Hurry up!" Her father swirled and glared at her so fiercely, Chloe stopped, astonished. He marched toward her and bent, his face just inches from hers; his breath, rank with the odor of stale alcohol, blowing over her in white smoky waves. Instinctively, she swatted the air in front of her nose.

The smack came with such ferocity she fell to the ground. She lay there, hand on cheek, eyes so wide they looked pure white. Unperturbed, he grabbed her by the shoulder of her coat and yanked her to her feet and boxed her ears with both hands. She ducked her head, trying to avoid the blows, until again, the power of his fists felled her and she crumpled in a heap on the soft bed of snow.

"Where's your hat!"

It was not a question and Chloe didn't dare respond.

Then came a strange male's voice, and another, and yet a third, and suddenly Chloe was surrounded by legs in blue jeans. She peeked from the ground and watched as three men from the nearby Christmas tree lot wedged their bodies between her and her father, forming a wall,

CHERYL CHUMLEY

and began shouting at him. She couldn't make out all their words, but she heard her father's cursing and then shortly after, she saw one of the men duck and step sharply to the side, narrowly avoiding a fist to the jaw. About that time, a woman in a blue puffy jacket kneeled by Chloe's side and whispered that it was time to leave.

"What's your name?" The woman had the kindest face Chloe had ever seen. "Chloe? Okay, Chloe. How about if you let me take you home now? Would that be okay with you?"

Chloe strained to see over the woman's shoulder to her father, but all she could make out was a mass of coats and legs, moving about rapidly.

"My husband and his friends there—" and the woman tilted back her head over her shoulder to indicate the men who surrounded her father, "will get your father home. He shouldn't be driving. It seems maybe he's had a little too much to drink?"

She said it like a question but also an accusation, and Chloe looked at her sharply, poised to say something sarcastic. But the woman smiled so gently and with such compassion, Chloe felt a lump form in her throat and all she could manage was a nod. Every Christmas, it was something, and for a brief moment, Chloe looked wistfully at a young girl, about the same age of twelve or thirteen, standing next to a man who had to have been her father, as they laughed and watched as their Christmas tree was loaded onto the top of their vehicle. The man pulled out some bills and handed them to the boy who strapped down their tree, then he placed a hand on the shoulder of the girl as he helped her into the car. It was the way he guided her into the front seat that grabbed at Chloe's heart. It was as if he were loading in a precious possession, taking all the time in the world to help buckle her seat belt and check to make sure she was

HECTOR

properly fastened. Chloe was lucky if her dad was sober when he drove.

She now looked at the cold faces of Juan and Romo and thought maybe Hector's dad had been the kind who made sure Hector was buckled properly before driving.

That's how James described his situation, anyway—Hector's parents were loving and warm, raising their son as a Christian, and his life had been happy.

And then it was all snatched from him, she thought, biting hard as she turned from the television screen to James.

"We should go find him," she said.

James stared, then nodded in agreement.

"Yes, we should, Chloe."

They sniffed at the same time, and both their expressions turned to wonder. James spoke it first.

"Roses."

❄ ❄ ❄

"I have no idea where else to look. Do you?"

Chloe shook her head in frustration. They had been driving for hours, scouring the streets, checking the local shelters, even stopping by the hospitals and local medical clinics on the off chance Hector had perhaps sought health care for some reason. Short of getting out of their car and searching down dark, dangerous alleyways or finding homeless people to query, Chloe couldn't think of anywhere else she and James could look.

"I guess we can keep driving around?" She glanced at his face for reaction. "Or maybe go back to the church and see if he's come back?"

James sighed and nibbled his bottom lip, weaving slowly through the parking lot to the back of the stores. He strained his neck to see behind the trash bins as he drove by them.

"You look in the wooded areas there," he said, pointing past Chloe's face to her passenger window. "Maybe he's hiding there." James cleared his throat and braked, squinting as he peered at a group of trash bins. Seeing nothing, he let up on the brake and pressed lightly on the gas, sighing loudly as the engine gunned and he rounded the side of the buildings toward the front lot again.

"Remember, he probably doesn't know about Romo and Juan. He probably doesn't know the latest police news. So he's going to be hiding out, thinking they're looking for him."

Chloe let out a long breath, imagining Hector, afraid and alone, in fear of being found by the cartel. Idly, lost in thought, she barely noticed the car had come to a stop.

"What's that your singing?" James pulled the key out of the ignition and turned to her with a smile. "I once was lost, but now I'm found? Amazing Grace?"

Chloe shook her head and laughed.

"I guess I was," she said, embarrassed.

She watched as James opened his door and stepped out, then did the same. They leaned almost simultaneously against the hood of the car, then stretched back so their heads were angled at the sky. Far above, a bird slowly circled, its dark wings flat, like two motionless propellers. They watched in silence as the bird drew closer, dropping in almost even increments a few feet at a time, while circling, circling, continuously circling. Its motion was mesmerizing and as it drew near, its black feathers glowed and they could see something shiny dangling from its beak. James was just about to say something; in fact, he impulsively grabbed onto Chloe's arm as his body stiffened in excitement. . But a flash of silver cut through the air and all that came from his mouth was a surprised, "Oh!" He bent to

HECTOR

the ground and then, with trembling fingers, extended his hand toward Chloe's face.

She looked and her expression turned to utter shock.

There, swinging gently in the air, was James's chain, upon which was spinning in tiny circles a shiny Christian cross pendant.

"Caww!"

The call of the crow as it flapped away startled Chloe and as she turned to watch its flight, a slumped figure on the curb by the grassy edge of the lot grabbed her attention. She nudged James and pointed.

Then the both gasped. There, sitting dejectedly, head hung low, was Hector.

"What the—" James let the words trail off as he first slowly and hesitantly, and then with purpose, walked toward him.

At the sound of approaching footsteps, Hector raised his head, his eyes in a tight squint. He hastily started to rise, as if preparing to flee. Then a look of recognition spread across his face and his mouth broke into a wide smile. Chloe watched as his arms encircled James, and she breathed in deeply, fighting off tears.

The glitter from the cross James still grasped in his hands flashed and gleamed and as she watched it dance, Chloe started to chuckle.

You do work in mysterious ways, she said softly, looking to the sky and shaking her head very slightly several times. *You really do work in mysterious ways.*

A preview of Book Three of the Chloe's People series

LILLY

"How do you spell your first name?"

Lilly sighed. It was the question she most hated—and the one she was asked most frequently.

"Double 'Ls,'" she said, holding up two fingers to make a "V" shape in the air. "Like the peace sign."

The girl looked up quizzically from her desk, her pen poised above the paper. Instead of smiling, she scrunched her face. Lilly sighed again.

"Double 'Ls.' L-I-L-L-Y," she said, her tone dripping with boredom. Lilly paused, waiting for a reaction, and when she received none, she tightened her lips to hide a smile and continued. "And S-M-I-T-H. That's how you spell Smith. That's how you spell my last name." She hoped the girl caught her condescending tone. But if she had, she didn't let on. Her face expressionless, the girl turned her head back to the paper and for the next few moments, the only sounds were the *click-click* of a pen tapping on wood and the soft rub of her wrist sliding across the paper as she scribbled furiously to fill in all the empty boxes.

She finished and shoved the sheet roughly toward Lilly.

"Read here. Initial here. Then turn it over to sign," she said, tapping loudly with her pen at several spots on the page. The sharpness of the pen point smacking on the desk irritated Lilly, and she answered as rudely as she could.

"Got a pen?" She sniffed loudly and grimaced.

LILLY

I'm the friggin' patient, Lilly thought, staring hard at the top of the girl's head as she waited. After several moments, she finally held out a pen without looking up and Lilly grabbed at it, feeling a stab of satisfaction when she felt her fingernail strike the girl's palm. She hoped it left a mark.

Some people just shouldn't be receptionists, she thought, sniffing again and squinting hard at the small print.

The medical terms made no sense to her and neither did the legal jargon. After finding herself reading the same sentence for the fourth time with no success and then glancing at the receptionist's blank face and deciding it would be no use to ask for clarification, Lilly shrugged.

Oh well, she thought, skipping reading and firing off her initials in rapid time as she scoured for the blank lines the receptionist noted with black "x" marks. She clamped her lips together tightly, as if in effort to stop herself from talking, then flipped the paper to finish with her full signature. *After today,* she thought absently, *what will it matter?* With a mix of resignation and exasperation, she sighed then pushed the tip of the pen hard against the page.

She was just about to sign her name—in fact, she had already started—when a loud bang startled her and she shot to her feet, turning toward the door. The paper flew off the desk and floated to the floor, the "y" of her half-finished signature trailing off like a jerky spasm in contrast to the other neatly aligned letters. She only half noticed the others in the waiting room, some of whom were now standing too, all staring with open mouths, in various states of surprise.

"Jesus saves!" A woman with disheveled hair and a long pink jacket stood in the foyer, shaking a poster board furiously back and forth, back and forth. "Jesus saves!"

A rush of blue clothing swept across Lilly's line of vision as three nurses dressed in hospital scrubs emerged from beyond

CHERYL CHUMLEY

a closed door and converged on the woman, surrounding her and yelling out unintelligible phrases. Lilly watched the mass of arms and hands grabbing at the woman, at her poster board, at her coat sleeve. The woman's green knit hat fell to the floor and skidded several feet, coming to rest at the foot of a square coffee table stacked high with magazines.

"Jesus saves!"

The woman rattled the poster board as best she could, raising it high above her head to keep it from the clutches of the nurse. Lilly could see it was filled with photographs taped in neat little rows. At first, she couldn't make out the subjects, but then her eyes caught sight of one of the labels beneath a picture. It read "12 WEEKS," and suddenly, Lilly understood. The photos were of various stages of development of fetuses in the womb. And as she stared hard at the one corresponding with "12 WEEKS," and took in the orange-colored image in which was clearly nestled a baby, albeit teeny, with an oversize head and tiny hands, she gulped. Involuntarily, her own hand moved to her belly. She left it there, fingers outstretched, feeling the slight swell of her abdomen and wondering if right below the surface of her skin, right beneath the slight caressing of her palm, were a baby's hands.

"Damn Jesus freaks!"

The receptionist's angry outburst jolted Lilly back to the present, and she dropped her hand. The nurses were pushing the woman out the front door, but she wasn't going quietly and all the while, shaking her poster board high above her head, frantically twisting it so the photos might face those in the waiting room.

"You don't have to do this! Jesus saves!"

For the briefest moment, the woman's and Lilly's eyes locked. It was only for a second, maybe two, but in that

LILLY

short time Lilly felt a surge of heat course through her body so intense she had to grab ahold of a nearby chair to keep from falling. It was as if the woman was speaking directly to her. More than that—it was as if the woman was reading her mind.

"Those demons are lying to you." For a split second, all motion stopped and it was just Lilly and the woman, staring into each other's eyes, and the only sound was the deepness of her voice from across the room. Shocked, Lilly gasped.

How does she know about them?

Then the moment passed and the woman's eyes were gone, swallowed in blue scrubs and disappeared with the rest of her body through the front door. The shouts of the nurses quickly died down, as they glanced triumphantly at the faces of young women scattered about the waiting room. Then they dropped their heads and walked quickly, one pausing to pick up the poster board that had been wrenched from the woman's hands. Lilly watched as the nurse tore it into tiny pieces, then crumpled the pieces into even tinier balls. Their voices, as they walked, sounded an exaggerated fury in the otherwise silent office.

"Can you believe the gall—"

"We should have called the police on—"

"I thought we were supposed to have security to deal with—"

Their voices faded as they disappeared behind a metal door marked "Patients and Staff ONLY," and as the latch clicked, it was as if a switch had been flipped, signifying a return to normalcy. The waiting room suddenly bustled with activity as women scraped their chairs to settle into their seats, and teenage girls resumed flipping through the pages of magazines they only pretended to read. Lilly turned back to the desk, her pen still in hand.

"Oh," she said softly, looking about for her paper then stooping to retrieve it from the floor. Her eyes fell on a crumpled piece of poster board that had apparently fallen from the nurse's hands and rolled across the floor near her feet. She unrolled it slowly, then angled the image so she could view it clearly.

Her breath caught in her throat.

Staring back at her was the exact image of the fetus in the womb labeled, "12 WEEKS."

Lilly's hand shook slightly as she stared at the toes, so well formed she could count to ten.

"Are you signing or what?" The receptionist's brusque tone interrupted Lilly's count, and she flashed the girl a look of disdain.

The woman's odd remark about demons jumped to Lilly's mind and she shuddered, an icy coldness rippling across her back.

Last evening had been the worst. The shadows on the wall kept her from sleeping most of the night.

Lilly looked in the receptionist's eyes. They were dull and black and stared back unblinking, waiting. They reminded Lilly of something, but she couldn't think what. She struggled to pull in the memory.

"Next!"

From the corner of the room, Lilly saw a young girl rise from her chair and follow the nurse to the metal door. She looked scared. She couldn't have been more than fifteen or sixteen years old, Lilly thought. She wondered if she had seen the demons too.

TO BE CONTINUED . . .

If you haven't already, you'll want to read *Chloe*, the first of the *Chloe's People* saga

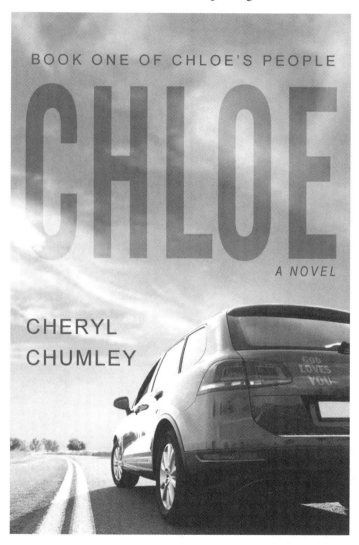

Chloe: Book One of Chloe's People A Novel
9781956454598 / 9781956454604 eBook

Other Fiction from Fidelis Publishing

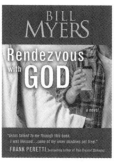

Rendezvous with God—
Volume One—Bill Myers
9781735428581 Paperback /
9781735428598 eBook

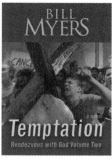

Temptation—Rendezvous with God—
Volume Two—Bill Myers
9781956454024 Paperback /
9781956454031 eBook

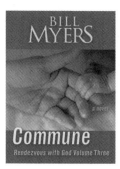

Commune: Rendezvous with God—
Volume Three—Bill Myers
9781956454246 Paperback /
9781956454253 eBook

Insight—Rendezvous with God—
Volume Four—Bill Myers
9781956454420 Paperback /
9781956454437 eBook

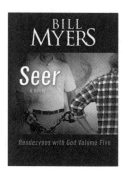

Seer—Rendezvous with God—
Volume Five—Bill Myers
9781956454574 /
9781956454581 eBook

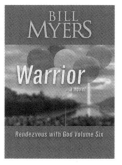

Warrior—Rendezvous with God—
Volume Six—Bill Myers
9781956454635 /
9781956454642 eBook

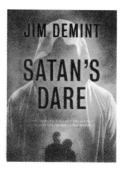

Satan's Dare—Jim DeMint
9781735856308 Hardcover /
9781735856315 eBook

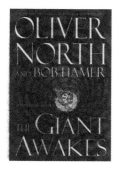

The Giant Awakes: A Jake Kruse Novel—
Oliver North and Bob Hamer
9781956454048 Hardcover /
9781956454055 eBook

*A Bellwether Christmas:
A Story Inspired by True
Events*—Laurel Guillen
9781956454086 Hardcover /
9781956454093 eBook

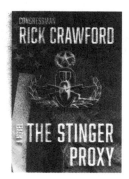

The Stinger Proxy—
Rick Crawford
9781956454215 Hardcover /
9781956454222 eBook

The Inferno—Winston Brady
9781956454260 Paperback /
9781956454277 eBook

*The Invisible War: Tribulation
Cult Book 1*—Michael Phillips
9781956454321 Paperback /
9781956454338 eBook